Photography by **ART WOLFE**

PRimates

THE AMAZING WORLD OF LEMURS, MONKEYS, AND APES

Text by Barbara Sleeper

Foreword by Dr. Russell A. Mittermeier

CHRONICLE BOOKS

SAN FRANCISCO

Text copyright © 1997 by Barbara Sleeper.
Photographs/Illustrations copyright © 1997 by Art Wolfe.

Library of Congress Cataloging-in-Publication Data:
    Sleeper, Barbara.
            Primates : the amazing world of lemurs,
monkeys, and apes / text by Barbara Sleeper ; photographs by
Art Wolfe; foreword by Dr. Russell A. Mittermeier.
            p.   cm.
            Includes bibliographical references and
index.   1. Primates.   I. Title.
        QL737.P9S54   1997
        599.8—dc21   97-979 CIP

ISBN 0-8118-1434-3

Printed in Hong Kong.

Cover and book design: Martine Trélaün

Photo on page 11: Haroldo Castro
Photo on page 13: Gavriel Jecan
Photo on page 15: Tom Boyden

Distributed in Canada by Raincoast Books
8680 Cambie Street
Vancouver, British Columbia V6P 6M9

10 9 8 7 6 5 4 3 2 1

Chronicle Books
85 Second Street
San Francisco, California 94105

Web Site: www.chronbooks.com

AUTHOR'S DEDICATION

In memory of Dr. Warren G. Kinzey, whose dedication to primatology, commitment to conservation, encouragement of students, remarkable athleticism in the field—and friendship—will remain a great source of inspiration.

O ver the past five years, and especially since the Earth Summit in Rio de Janeiro in 1992, conservation of biological diversity, the sum total of all life on our planet, has finally taken its rightful place on the global stage. A Biodiversity Convention, a major World Bank-based Global Environmental Facility focusing heavily on biodiversity, and a growing number of foundations and conservation organizations with biodiversity as their principal objective have raised the profile of this key issue and channeled funding in its direction.

The entire planet's biodiversity is of great importance, but clearly certain groups of species and a small number of particularly rich ecosystems, mainly in the tropics, deserve special attention. Among these are the nonhuman primates, the monkeys, apes, lemurs, lorises, galagos, and tarsiers that are our closest living relatives. Not only are these animals intriguing unto themselves, they occupy a very special position in the imagination of our own primate species, *Homo sapiens.*

As research over the past four decades has shown, nonhuman primates can teach us a great deal about ourselves and our evolution. For example, they have played an important, if highly controversial, role in biomedical research since the development of the polio vaccine in the 1950s, and they have been critical in helping us to understand what early humans must have been like. The continuing growth of primatology and primate-oriented anthropological research clearly demonstrates that our interest in our closest relatives is not likely to wane anytime soon.

Aside from the ways in which primates can enlighten us about ourselves, primate field research has intrinsic value—it provides valuable information relevant to tropical ecology. About 90 percent of all primates are found in the world's tropical rain forests. These habitats are the richest and most diverse terrestrial ecosystems, and the primates living in them play a very important role, as seed dispersers, seed predators, and even pollinators. The role of larger rain forest species like the Amazonian spider and woolly monkeys as seed dispersers seems to be especially critical to the maintenance of forest structure and diversity.

Unfortunately, wild populations of nonhuman primates are in trouble in all of the ninety-two countries in which they live. The most serious problems are in those nations richest in primates, including Brazil, Peru, Colombia, Madagascar, Zaire, Indonesia, China, and Vietnam. Primates are threatened by the destruction of their forests and other natural habitats, by hunting as food (especially severe in West and Central Africa and parts of Amazonia), and by live capture for export, although the impact of this threat has declined considerably in recent years.

As a result, of the roughly two hundred and seventy-five species of nonhuman primates currently known, about half are considered of "conservation concern" by the World Conservation Union (IUCN) Primate Specialist Group. Of these, one in five is already in either the endangered or critical category, meaning that they could go extinct in the next couple of decades. Although we will probably come through this century without having lost a single primate species or subspecies (which can't be said for most other major groups of vertebrates), we will enter the next millennium with a large number of primate species on the edge.

To prevent the extinction of a significant percentage of our primate relatives, a wide variety of actions is needed now. High on the list is the need for more accurate information. We are still amazingly ignorant about the basic issues of geographic distribution and taxonomy (scientific classification) for most primate species, to the point that we are still discovering new species almost every year.

The most striking examples of new discoveries over the past decade have been in Madagascar and Brazil. In Madagascar, two distinctive new species, the golden bamboo lemur and Tattersall's sifaka, were found and described in the late 1980s. A third species, the pygmy mouse lemur described more than one hundred years ago and forgotten, is not only still alive, but quite distinct. This rediscovered species is now considered the world's smallest living primate.

In Brazil, the record for new species discoveries is even more striking. Six new species have been discovered and described since 1990. These include *Leontopithecus caissara, Callithrix nigriceps, Cebus kaapori, Callithrix mauesi, Callithrix marcai,* and the most recent, *Callithrix saterei.* A seventh is in the process of being described, and there may also be four to five others.

Discoveries continue in other parts of the world as well. A new form of colobus monkey was recently identified in the Niger Delta of Africa, and several new galago taxa have surfaced in the past few years. In addition to these spectacular discoveries, almost every field research expedition now obtains significant new information on geographic distribution, range extensions, and so on.

Efforts to conserve primates have been underway for the past twenty years. Of particular note are the activities of the Primate Specialist Group of the World Conservation Union's (IUCN) Species Survival Commission (SSC). This group, with some three hundred members worldwide, first produced a Global Strategy for Primate Conservation in 1978. This was followed by the development of a series of primate conservation Action Plans for Africa, Asia, Madagascar, and Mesoamerica, which have had considerable impact. The Primate Specialist Group also issues a yearly journal, **PRIMATE CONSERVATION**, and has regional newsletters **(NEOTROPICAL PRIMATES, ASIAN PRIMATES, AFRICAN PRIMATES,** and **LEMUR NEWS)** that reach a broad primate conservation community. Through its action plans and other activities, the group has attracted millions of dollars to the field since 1977 and continues to be a catalyst for conservation activities.

A number of other organizations have played major roles in primate conservation, including the Wildlife Conservation Society (WCS), Conservation International (CI), the World Wildlife Fund (WWF), the African Wildlife Foundation (AWF), Jersey Wildlife Preservation Trust (JWPT), the Dian Fossey Gorilla Fund, the Jane Goodall Institute, and a number of zoos, including the Brookfield Zoo, the Columbus Zoo, the Cincinnati Zoo, and several others. A new foundation, the Margot Marsh Biodiversity Foundation, is dedicated exclusively to primates.

In spite of all this support and activity, there have been gaps in primatology. The lack of quality publications for the general public, especially books depicting these amazing creatures and their great diversity, is one glaring example. When most people think about primates, they think only of chimps, gorillas, baboons, and maybe the occasional capuchin monkey. But the Order Primates, the taxonomic classification of mammals that includes all lemurs, monkeys, apes, and humans, is wonderfully diverse in ways that few people recognize. Those of us in the conservation community are especially interested in portraying this rich diversity and helping to stimulate public concern for disappearing primates. Top-notch publications play a critical role in our efforts to spread our message as widely as possible.

I am therefore very pleased to introduce this excellent book by world-class photographer Art Wolfe. Art's photography is simply spectacular, and all of his photos are new for this book, including some of species rarely captured by the camera. Art's photography and Barbara Sleeper's excellent text combine to give us a real feel for the great diversity of species contained within this unique mammalian order.

Among the book's most attractive features are a geographic breakdown of the four major regions in which primates live: Madagascar, Africa, Asia, and the Neotropical region (including Mexico, Central and South America), and the strong focus on the primates of the most critical countries for global primate conservation, including Brazil (with 76 species), Madagascar (with 32 species), Indonesia (with 36 species), and Zaire (with 37 species). Although wild primates inhabit ninety-two countries, these four alone are responsible for almost 70 percent of all primate species. This is not to say that the other eighty-eight countries in which primates live are not important—indeed, they are. But we must concentrate a significant portion of our conservation effort on the countries that contain the greatest number of species. Only by doing so can we hope to preserve the overall diversity of the Order Primates of which we form an integral part.

Madagascar, generally acknowledged as the world's highest primate conservation priority, shows the importance of a strategically focused effort to conserve primates. With its unmatched endemism, Madagascar ranks third on the world list of primate species diversity, yet is less than 7 percent of the size of Brazil, the world leader, and roughly one-quarter the size of Indonesia or Zaire, which rank second and fourth, respectively. Madagascar's thirty-two species and fifty distinct taxa are 100 percent endemic. Two species, *Eulemur fulvus* and *Eulemur mongoz*, also live on the nearby Comoro Islands, but they were almost certainly introduced there from Madagascar.

At the family and generic levels, Madagascar's primate diversity is even more striking, with fully five primate families and fourteen genera found nowhere else. Compare this to Brazil, the richest country on Earth in primate species with seventy-six, but with only three families, none of them endemic, and two endemic genera out of sixteen. And of the fifty lemur taxa recognized for Madagascar, fully ten are considered critically endangered, seven are endangered, and another nineteen vulnerable. In addition, one entire family (Daubentoniidae) and four genera are considered endangered. This represents a degree of primate endangerment at higher taxonomic levels unmatched by any other country and is of great international concern.

Look at Madagascar's diversity in yet another way: Although it is only one of ninety-two countries to have wild primate populations, it alone is home to 13 percent of all primate species (32 species of 275 species total), 23 percent of all primate genera (14 genera of 65 genera total), and 36 percent of all primate families (5 families of 14 families total), which is a great responsibility for any one nation.

Madagascar also demonstrates that the possibility of primate extinctions is not a figment of the conservationists' imagination. Fully eight genera and at least fifteen species of lemur have already gone extinct on this island since the arrival of our own species there less than two thousand years ago, and many others could disappear within the next few decades if rapid action is not taken.

In summary, a lot of work needs to be done if primates in countries such as Madagascar are to continue to enrich our lives and teach us about ourselves. More books like this one are urgently needed to stimulate interest in conservation both in the United States and in the tropical countries where so many of this planet's animals and plants live. I am delighted to have had an opportunity to participate in making this book a reality.

Finally, it is an honor to be part of a book dedicated to one of the century's great primatologists, my good friend the late Warren G. Kinzey. Warren was one of the true pioneers of primatology and a wonderfully modest, always enthusiastic man whose wide-ranging accomplishments from the laboratory to the remote corners of Amazonia are sorely missed by those who remember his work. A beautiful book like this on the animals to which he devoted his life is a fitting tribute.

RUSSELL A. MITTERMEIER, Ph.D.

CHAIRMAN,
IUCN/SSC Primate Specialist Group,
and President,
Conservation International

Every photographer's dream is to photograph under authentic and wild conditions, to capture the rarest of the rare, to reach the most difficult to find, and to document never-before-seen behavior. All require some degree of exposure, access, and disturbance to the subjects and their environment.

I have always been concerned with the delicate balancing act between the art of photography and the welfare of the wildlife at the other end of the lens; habitats are easily disturbed and the animals themselves are often endangered by careless humans prying into their lives. However, I, like many others, have been thrilled by the romance of the chase and the journey to seek out rare and beautiful creatures. To photograph **PRIMATES**, I traveled to Rwanda's lush Parc des Volcans for mountain gorillas, to Uganda's deep forests of Kibale National Park for colobus monkeys and gray-cheeked mangabeys, to Borneo's rain forests for orangutans, to Madagascar's endangered forests for lemurs, and to Japan's tranquil Yakushima Island for snow monkeys.

Throughout my career, I have worked with an impressive group of field biologists, wildlife management professionals, researchers, and conservation organizations involved in comprehensive studies of primates both in the wild and in captivity. They, in turn, led me on a search of special captive collections. Excellent programs abound throughout the world, and I soon discovered an amazingly large circle of well-organized, dedicated, and efficiently networked professionals, all striving for the same goal of primate conservation and public education. Without their efforts, access to these mammals, both wild and rare in species, would have been nearly impossible and extremely restricted.

Over the last few years I have worked on many natural history books, including **WILD CATS OF THE WORLD, OWLS: THEIR LIFE AND BEHAVIOR,** and **PRIMATES**. Following the leads of researchers and biologists, I embarked on a worldwide adventure in search of special private and public animal collections to photograph for these books. The research and planning required to locate these special collections and gain authorization to photograph them was often more chal-

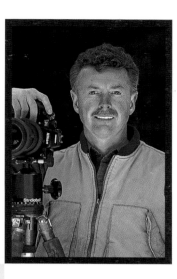

lenging than the skill required to photograph animals in the wild. In many cases, an extremely rare animal in the wild was just as difficult to find in captivity. The red uakari is an excellent example of this, as only a handful exist in captivity.

Working in captive conditions presents its own photographic challenges: subpar lighting, gated, fenced, and glass enclosures, the curious public, and strict rules designed to protect the animals. Zoos serve many purposes, including conservation, education, and breeding. An additional but no less important purpose is less well known: Zoos are a means by which books, magazines, and educational publications are illustrated with animals. Endangered species benefit from pictures of their captive brethren. Not only are their wild kin not bothered in their wild habitats, but a strong image of a captive and flawless specimen brings attention to the animal and galvanizes support for the species. Tigers and wolves are good examples. The public can't get enough of engaging close-up photographs of these two animals, yet it is quite dangerous for both the photographer and the subject to achieve this in the wild.

PRIMATES was a memorable project for me to work on. The primates themselves made fascinating subjects. Their undeniable resemblance to humans is the principal reason for this. Their keen intelligence was obvious and left me respectful. I have many fond and vivid memories of the time spent photographing my nonhuman relatives. I will never forget having my East African camp raided repeatedly by clever vervet monkeys and baboons, or being adopted by a baby woolly monkey in the Peruvian Amazon, who never left my neck without a toothy protest. And I will not forget the devoted individuals I met working on this book—scientists, park officials, zookeepers, among others—all fiercely protective of these remarkable creatures and steadfast in their support. This book is dedicated to them and to the primates and their habitats they have committed their lives to studying and protecting.

ART WOLFE

Nonhuman primates live in ninety-two countries around the world. Approximately sixty-five genera and two hundred and seventy-five species (including *Homo sapiens*) have been recognized. From Asia's hooting gibbons and nocturnal slow loris, to Africa's colorful guenons, the majority of all primates are arboreal forest-dwellers that inhabit the world's remaining rain forests. A few exceptions include the terrestrial baboons and patas monkeys of Africa, and the hefty gorillas that prefer to spend their time on the ground.

While most people are very familiar with gorillas, chimps, and orangutans, referred to as the great apes, less known are the myriad species of smaller primates. From South America's tiny pygmy marmoset that can fit inside a teacup, to the medium- or cat-sized titi monkeys which live in tail-twining, monogamous family groups, primates come in all sizes and colors. For example, Madagascar's pygmy mouse lemur, which weighs just one ounce, is considered the smallest of all living primates. In contrast, adult male mountain gorillas are the largest, tipping the scales at 400 pounds or more.

The primate conservation community recognizes four major geographic regions in which primates live, with no overlap among them. These four regions include the island of Madagascar, designated as a special primate biogeographic region unto itself; the entire continent of Africa; south and Southeast Asia, with a handful of species in temperate Asia; and the Neotropical region encompassing Mexico and Central and South America.

Nonhuman primates are often referred to as Old World and New World monkeys. The Old World monkeys include most of the species native to Africa and Asia, including Africa's guenons, talapoin monkeys, baboons, and colobus monkeys, and Asia's langurs and macaques. New World monkeys, such as the woolly, spider, titi, howler, and capuchin monkeys, live only in the Neotropics (or "new" tropics) of Mexico and Central and South America. Anatomical as well as geographical differences distinguish Old World from New World monkeys.

Prosimians are another distinct group of primates. While the word *simian* refers to all higher monkeys and apes, *prosimian* refers to the more primitive primates—the lemurs, lorises, pottos, and bushbabies. Anatomically, prosimians differ from the higher primates by having relatively longer snouts, more teeth, and lower jaws comprised of not one, but two separate bones joined by cartilage. Lemurs are native to Madagascar, while pottos and bushbabies live in Africa. The lorises live in Asia. The majority of all prosimians are nocturnal, with the exception of Madagascar's large diurnal lemurs.

Toward the top of the evolutionary tree, gibbons and siamangs have been designated as lesser apes; chimpanzees, orangutans, and gorillas as great apes. From there a trail of early hominid ancestors has led to the evolution of *Homo sapiens*.

While not inclusive, the following photographic collection of 102 primate species from around the world has been selected for this book to show the phenomenal diversity in size, coloration, habitat preference, and social structure of the Order Primates. While the beautiful photographs let the subjects speak for themselves—of their innate curiosity, intelligence, and dignity—the accompanying natural history text is meant to give an overview of the fascinating social behavior, ecology, and critical habitat requirements that characterize our closest living nonhuman relatives—the primates.

The species presented here are grouped according to the four geographic areas in which they live. Within each region, the species are listed from the most primitive—lemurs, lorises, pottos, bushbabies, and tarsiers—to the more evolutionarily advanced—monkeys and apes. Although we, too, belong to the Order Primates, descriptions of *Homo sapiens* have intentionally been omitted from this book in an effort to concentrate on our engaging nonhuman relatives.

BARBARA SLEEPER

Mada

This once-isolated island nation is by far one of the most unique areas for primate evolution and conservation. While only 7 percent the size of Brazil and roughly one-quarter the size of Indonesia or Zaire, Madagascar contains an amazing fourteen genera and thirty-two species of primates. Most important, all are endemic, meaning they occur nowhere else on Earth.

From the legendary aye-aye and ghostlike indri to the leaping, vocal sifakas and the more familiar ring-tailed lemurs, Madagascar is home to a remarkable assortment of primates. Not only does this make Madagascar a coveted travel destination for those cultivating a "life list" of primate species, but it puts a tremendous conservation burden on the Malagasy government to balance human needs with wildlife needs.

The fossil record proves that primate extinction has already happened. Madagascar's current primate diversity is nothing compared to what existed 1,500 to 2,000 years ago when humans first arrived on the island. At that time twenty-two genera and forty-seven primate species were still alive, including a species of lemur that grew larger than an adult male gorilla. Since then, an estimated 85 percent of the island's tropical forests have been slashed and burned for wood and agricultural land. The badly eroded, nutrient-depleted soils threaten the remaining forests. As a result, roughly 70 percent of the island's endemic primate population is in some type of trouble, with several species on the verge of extinction.

GRAY MOUSE LEMUR

(Microcebus murinus)

Because of their small size and ability to thrive in altered habitats, mouse lemurs are one of the most abundant, widespread species of lemurs in Madagascar. Only a few forests do not contain them. With elongated bodies and short legs, these nocturnal omnivores move on all fours over the tree branches to feed on insects and small vertebrates such as chameleons, frogs, and geckos. They also eat gum and sap, and flowers, fruit, and leaves. During the day they curl up to sleep in small nests made from dead leaves or in holes in trees. Weighing only two to three ounces (seasonally), mouse lemurs are one of the smallest living lemurs, and are among the smallest of all primates. Females usually give birth to twins in November and carry their offspring around in their mouths for the first three weeks of the babies' lives.

△ A gray mouse lemur peers from its nest in a tree hole. These tiny, nocturnal prosimians move quadrupedally on short legs through the forest's tree canopy, feeding on insects and small vertebrates.

COQUEREL'S DWARF LEMUR
(Mirza coquereli)

Native to Madagascar's western dry deciduous forests, Coquerel's dwarf lemur holds the distinction of being the only species within the genus *Mirza*. Both dental features and behavioral traits distinguish this species from other dwarf lemurs. Weighing a little less than ten ounces, or three times as much as a mouse lemur, this nocturnal prosimian has large ears and eyes ideal for pursuing a diet of fruit, flowers, insects, frogs, and chameleons at night. Rapid quadrupedal running over branches best describes its preferred locomotion through the forest.

◊ **The Coquerel's dwarf lemur is an agile, night-active omnivore native to Madagascar. When not running on all fours through the forest canopy, it clings to tree trunks, hangs upside-down from branches, and leaps through the foliage.**

GREATER DWARF LEMUR
(Cheirogaleus major)

Greater dwarf lemurs inhabit the eastern rain forests of Madagascar, where they sleep in small groups by day and forage mostly alone at night. After dark, they vocalize with high-pitched whistling calls, thought to be territorial. As dwarf lemurs move through the trees in search of fruit, gums, and insects, they mark the branches with glandular secretions. As part of this olfactory communication, they also deposit cylindrical trails of feces that differ from their normal pattern of defecation. Greater dwarf lemurs build up fat deposits in their tails to help carry them through the southern winter from July to September.

▽ **A greater dwarf lemur quietly navigates through the trees of Madagascar. Because of its large range, small size, and nocturnal habits, it is one of the least endangered of the Malagasy lemurs.**

FAT-TAILED DWARF LEMUR

(Cheirogaleus medius)

There is a reason that the fat-tailed dwarf lemur of Madagascar has a pudgy appendage. This species hibernates for up to six months each year in the dry winter months, metabolizing the fat reserves in its tail and body until the rains return in November. Solitary foragers by night and communal dozers by day, as many as five of these little lemurs will share a tree hole. Measuring just sixteen to twenty inches from head to tail, this wide-ranging species inhabits the dry deciduous forests of western and southern Madagascar.

⌂ A fat-tailed dwarf lemur clings to a tree trunk in western Madagascar. This nocturnal omnivore eats fruit and flowers, as well as insects and small vertebrates such as chameleons. Its small size, large geographic distribution, and complete disappearance during a six-month hibernation have helped preserve this species.

GRAY BAMBOO LEMUR
(Hapalemur griseus)

Weighing up to two pounds, gray bamboo lemurs of Madagascar live in small, monogamous family groups of an adult pair with their young. They produce a variety of sounds, including contact calls between mother and young, mating calls between the sexes, group cohesive calls, and loud "kree" or alarm calls. These small lemurs live wherever reeds or bamboo grow, in the swampy areas and bamboo thickets of Madagascar. Their teeth are specialized for removing the outer sheath of bamboo stalks.

⇧ A white-footed sportive lemur from Madagascar peers from its daytime sleeping hole. Big eyes indicate that this species is nocturnal. At night these one-pound vegetarians leap through the canopy in search of leaves and flowers.

⇩ A gray bamboo lemur does the splits on a horizontal branch. With hindlimbs much longer than forelimbs, these endangered lemurs prefer vertical resting postures. They are built to leap easily between vertical bamboo stalks.

WHITE-FOOTED SPORTIVE LEMUR
(Lepilemur leucopus)

To date, seven species of sportive lemurs are recognized. Very little is known about most of these medium-sized lemurs, and debate continues about their taxonomic division. All are nocturnal, vertical clingers and leapers with elongated legs used to catapult through the canopy. Their range encircles the coastal forests of Madagascar, where the principal threat to their survival is loss of habitat to pastureland. Hunters use wooden traps to capture sportive lemurs for food. They also remove them from their daytime sleeping sites.

◊ **Named for its enormous black-and-white tail, the ring-tailed lemur spends as much time on the ground as it does in trees. Holding their tails aloft, ring-tails use their long, bushy appendages for dramatic visual signals.**

RING-TAILED LEMUR
(Lemur catta)

▽ **The fork of a tree provides a convenient place for a pile-up of ring-tailed lemurs. Although familiar to most people, this species is considered vulnerable in its wild habitat of Madagascar.**

Named for its eye-catching black-and-white tail, this day-active primate is one of the most terrestrial species of lemurs native to Madagascar. It is also probably the best known. Ring-tailed lemurs inhabit the dry scrub and deciduous and gallery forests of south and southwestern Madagascar, where they live in groups of three to twenty individuals. Females are dominant over males and remain in their birth groups. Infants begin riding on their mothers' backs within two weeks of birth. However, in spite of such close contact, only about 40 percent reach maturity. Ring-tailed lemurs use their banded tails for more than just visual signals. They also use them to "stink fight." After rubbing their tails in secretions from their wrist glands, they flick them at their rivals during conflicts.

Until 1988, the genus *Lemur* included the ring-tailed lemurs plus the five species now designated as *Eulemur* or true lemurs. DNA analysis prompted the reclassification.

◊ **A pair of ring-tailed lemurs *(Lemur catta)* mooch a banana from a willing ally in Madagascar.**

COMMON BROWN LEMUR
(Eulemur fulvus fulvus)

Weighing little more than five pounds, brown lemurs are distinctive for their lack of sexual dimorphism—both sexes look the same right down to their light beards and dark faces. Group size varies from three to twelve lemurs on the Madagascar mainland, and from two to twenty-nine on the Comoro Islands. The widespread distribution of this species is partly explained by their seasonally flexible diet of fruit, leaves, and flowers. They also show high rates of fiber digestion and an elevated tolerance for plant alkaloids and tannins. Researchers think such dietary flexibility helps reduce feeding competition within groups—and the need for female dominance.

▽ **Both sexes of Madagascar's common brown lemurs look alike. As is true for all lemur species, sense of smell is crucial. Their pointed muzzles with moist rhinaria (the area of naked skin surrounding the nostrils) help them pick up olfactory signals from each other.**

RED-FRONTED BROWN LEMUR

(Eulemur fulvus rufus)

The red-fronted brown lemur is found in the eastern and western deciduous forests of Madagascar. Depending on habitat, this tabby-sized prosimian shows a great deal of variability in its behavior. Western populations eat the leaves, flowers, bark, and sap from the kily tree. Eastern populations have been observed eating fruit, bird nests, insects, and dirt. Group size ranges from four to eighteen individuals. Red-fronted brown lemurs show a pattern of seasonal reproduction. They mate in June, give birth in September and October, and wean their young by January.

⌂ **One of the best places to see the red-fronted brown lemur is at the Ranomafana National Park in eastern Madagascar. Here, they move quadrupedally through the canopy feeding on plants.**

◁ **A Sanford's brown lemur from Madagascar is captured in portrait. Its restricted range, coupled with poaching, occasional brushfires, and tree cutting, have left this subspecies vulnerable.**

SANFORD'S BROWN LEMUR
(Eulemur fulvus sanfordi)

Active at night as well as by day, Sanford's brown lemur is restricted to the evergreen forests at the northernmost tip of Madagascar. Weighing nearly five pounds, these fruit-eating prosimians occasionally add invertebrate protein, including spiders, millipedes, and centipedes, to their mostly plant diet. Group size varies by habitat from three to fifteen individuals. The lavish off-white, cream, or slightly reddish ear tufts on the males help identify this subspecies in the wild.

▷ **Collared brown lemurs are members of the *Eulemur* genus, or true lemurs. Shared traits include sexual dichromatism (color differences between the sexes), quadrupedal locomotion, a medium or cat-sized body build, and a preference for nocturnal activity.**

COLLARED BROWN LEMUR
(Eulemur fulvus collaris)

Found in southeastern Madagascar, the collared brown lemur remains somewhat of a mystery. Very little is known about the ecology or behavior of this subspecies. Habitat destruction is the primary threat to their long-term survival. They are also trapped for the local pet trade and hunted for food. Because of this, collared brown lemurs are considered vulnerable. They inhabit only one small protected area on the island.

BLACK LEMUR

(Eulemur macaco macaco)

Striking sexual dimorphism makes it difficult to confuse this five-pound, brown-eyed lemur with any other lemur species. The males are uniformly black, including their long ear tufts, while the female's dark dorsal coat is highlighted by deep rust sides and white ear tufts. Found in disturbed and undisturbed forests of northwestern Madagascar, black lemurs feed on ripe fruit, leaves, flowers, and an occasional insect. Group size ranges from two to fifteen individuals, with the average size about ten. Females give birth to a single young between September and November. Black lemurs are killed by humans when they raid crops and are sometimes poached in nature reserves. The best place to see a black lemur in the wild is on Madagascar's offshore island, Nosy Komba.

⌂ A male black lemur looks almost leopard-like as he dangles his limbs and tail from a tree branch in Madagascar. Females of this dichromatic species are dominant over males for limited resources such as ripe fruit and trees suitable for sleeping.

⌂ Peering over a tree branch in Madagascar, a female black lemur shows the flaming rust-colored fur and long white ear tufts that differentiate her from her all-black mate.

SCLATER'S BLACK LEMUR
(Eulemur macaco flavifrons)

Sclater's black lemurs are a yet-unstudied subspecies of black lemur native to the dry forests and coffee and citrus plantations of northwest Madagascar. Because they do not live in any protected areas, this blue-eyed subspecies is considered to be critically endangered because of hunting, trapping, and habitat destruction. Only hybrids with brown eyes occur in the southern part of the Manongarivo Special Reserve.

◊ **Nontufted ears and bright blue eyes identify this primate as a Sclater's black lemur from Madagascar. Not found in any protected areas, this critically endangered subspecies was given the highest priority conservation rating in 1992 by the World Conservation Union (IUCN) Primate Specialist Group.**

CROWNED LEMUR

(Eulemur coronatus)

Of the five species of the *Eulemur* genus, the crowned lemur is one of the smallest, weighing about four pounds. Male and female crowned lemurs do not look alike. The females have short, gray body hair and pale cheeks and throats while the males are covered with dark gray-brown hair and have dark tails and black noses. Their preferred habitat is the dry forests of Madagascar, where they eat fruit, young leaves, flowers, and insects. Although mostly diurnal, crowned lemurs also travel and feed at night. Vocalizations are used to maintain group contact while foraging.

◁ **A crowned lemur peers through a lush Madagascar canopy. The best place to see these prosimians in the wild is in the island's Montagne d'Ambre National Park or Ankarana Special Reserve.**

MONGOOSE LEMUR
(Eulemur mongoz)

Mongoose lemurs are medium-sized, sexually dichromatic prosimians native to northwestern Madagascar. Introduced populations also live on the Comoro Islands of Moheli and Anjouan. Olfactory communication in this species is well developed. Mongoose lemurs use the glands on their wrists, palms, elbows, soles, chest, face, and genitals to communicate location, gender, and reproductive state. During the dry season, they feed mostly on nectar, adding occasional flowers, leaves, and fruit.

◁ **The mongoose lemur of Madagascar adjusts its daily activity pattern to season and climate. With the onset of the dry season in June, it shifts from diurnal to nocturnal activity.**

◁ The boisterous alarm calls of Madagascar's black-and-white ruffed lemurs begin as a grunt and end as a roar. The females form the core of each group and cooperate to defend their territory.

BLACK-AND-WHITE RUFFED LEMUR

(Varecia variegata variegata)

Ruffed lemurs are the largest of the quadrupedal lemurs (those that move on all fours). Characteristics that distinguish them from other species are their loud, raucous calls, striking coloration, and ears "ruffed" with long, thick hair. Black-and-white ruffed lemurs inhabit the coastal rain forests of eastern Madagascar, where they are able to hang upside-down by their feet to reach edible morsels. They are the most frugivorous of any living lemur, feeding on nectar, seeds, and leaves when fruit isn't available. Hunting and habitat destruction have left this species endangered throughout its range.

▷ A black-and-white ruffed lemur displays the beautiful coloration and white ear ruffs characteristic of this species. Their bright yellow eyes are offset by otherwise dark faces.

RED RUFFED LEMUR
(Varecia variegata rubra)

Red ruffed lemurs are another critically endangered species of primates. They are restricted to the remaining forests of the Masoala Peninsula in northeastern Madagascar. Olfaction is well developed in these exclusively arboreal primates. Females normally give birth to twins, but births of three to five infants have also been reported. This seems possible, since female ruffed lemurs have three sets of nipples. In 1964, Masoala Nature Reserve, the only protected area in their limited range, was downlisted to permit logging. Red ruffed lemurs are also trapped and eaten as food. Efforts are now underway to reestablish a protected area for these endangered primates.

⬦ A red ruffed lemur displays the small white patch of fur on its neck that breaks up its otherwise flame-red coat. The only place to see this endangered primate in the wild is on Madagascar's Masoala Peninsula.

⬦ The red ruffed lemur is one of the most beautiful primates. Its deep rust-red fur offsets a jet-black face and extremities. In the sunlight, its coat looks like it is on fire.

VERREAUX'S SIFAKA

(Propithecus verreauxi verreauxi)

Verreaux's sifakas are diurnal prosimians that live in small groups of two to twelve individuals. Short forelimbs and long hindlimbs make it possible for sifakas to vertically cling and leap through their arboreal habitat. To digest their diet of plant cellulose, they rely on bacteria-aided fermentation. So efficient is their absorption of fluid from plant materials that the only water they supposedly drink is the early-morning dew, which they lick off their fur. At birth, infants are nearly hairless and have black skin.

△ A Verreaux's sifaka, native to Madagascar, appears to dance as it leaps and sidesteps bipedally over the ground

◁ The predominantly white fur with brown-capped white head identify this langorous primate as a Verreaux's sifak When active, its long legs are used for vertical clinging and leaping through the trees.

COQUEREL'S SIFAKA
(Propithecus verreauxi coquereli)

Covered with dense body hair, Coquerel's sifaka is distinguishable from other sifaka species by its all-white head and maroon chest and shoulder fur. Weighing nearly eight pounds, this diurnal leaper is found in evergreen and mixed deciduous forests in reserves in northwestern Madagascar. Infants are born during the months of June and July. During the first month, infants cling to the mother's chest. Soon after, they transfer to her back for acrobatic rides through the forest. The young reach adult size after one year. Sifakas use their long tails to help balance and steer as they move.

⌂ **This portrait of a Coquerel's sifaka shows the characteristic black face, white head, and blazing yellow eyes of this beautiful prosimian. Named for the loud "si-fak" calls it makes, the endangered Coquerel's sifaka is now restricted almost entirely to Madagascar's Ankarafantsika Nature Reserve and the Bora Special Reserve.**

GOLDEN-CROWNED or TATTERSALL'S SIFAKA
(Propithecus tattersalli)

INDRI
(Indri indri)

Considered another critically endangered lemur species from Madagascar, the golden-crowned sifaka was first formally described to science in 1988. Restricted to remnant forest patches in northern Madagascar, it has one of the smallest documented populations and limited distributions of all lemurs. This long-limbed, vertically leaping prosimian with protruding ears produces a clearly enunciated "si-fak!" call to warn of predators. Unprotected in any national park or wildlife reserve, this rare species continues to lose habitat to periodic brush fires and agriculture. They are also hunted for food.

◊ **A rare golden-crowned sifaka feeds on a leaf in a Madagascar forest. This species produces specific warning sounds to distinguish between avian and terrestrial predators.**

The indri is the largest lemur native to Madagascar (others that were larger are now extinct) and one of the most endangered. Its vestigial tail and large twelve-pound size distinguish it from all other species; so do its melodious, gibbon-like calls. The prominent ears are tufted and always black, while the size and location of the white fur patches on its otherwise black coat can vary by geographic location. Active by day, indris are vertical clingers and leapers that inhabit Madagascar's eastern rain forests. They live in small monogamous family groups dominated by the adult female. Territorial boundaries are demarcated with scent marks and defended vocally with loud howls and barks. Called "babakoto" by the people of Madagascar, the indri is included in many local creation stories about the origin of people. In Malagasy the name "indri" translates literally to "There it is!"

◊ **An indri clings to a tree in Madagascar. Its dramatic black-and-white coloration helps to break up its outline in the canopy.**

AYE-AYE

(Daubentonia madagascariensis)

Toothmarks on tree trunks and gnawed coconuts are a sure sign that an insect-hunting aye-aye is near. About the size of a housecat, with yellow eyes, grizzled brown fur, and long bony digits, the nocturnal aye-aye has been called both beautiful and ugly. Resembling an escapee from the film *Gremlins*, this strange-looking animal resembles no other primate on Earth. With oversized ears, a pinched face, puffy foxlike tail, and digits that look like witches' fingers, the aye-aye was first classified as a squirrel. It is another of the highly endangered members of the lemur group—classified in its own separate family.

Like a woodpecker, the aye-aye uses its mobile, batlike ears to listen for the sounds of beetle grubs hidden underneath tree bark. Once located, it tears into the bark with its four continuously growing incisors, then uses its long, skinny middle finger to probe the wood for soft grubs. Able to bend in every direction, even backward to touch its forearm, this specialized digit is used to tap tree trunks, poke holes in eggs, and extract milk from coconuts.

Aye-ayes are endangered due to habitat loss—and superstition. Legend has it that if an aye-aye points its bony third finger at you, you will die a swift and horrible death. As a result, many Malagasy villagers kill them on sight.

◠ The aye-aye, native to Madagascar, is highly endangered. Perfectly adapted for an arboreal life searching for fruit and grubs, the aye-aye's haunting face and bony fingers have caused it to be persecuted by fearful natives.

◊ In addition to its strange appearance, the aye-aye is the only primate with a single pair of mammae situated low on the abdomen.

◡ The aye-aye best exemplifies the "curse of the uncuddly." Its grisled hair, bat-like ears, and glow-in-the-dark nocturnal eyes have spooked many Malagasy people to this harmless primate, rather than endearing it to them.

AFR

From the small, nocturnal, branch-leaping galagos to the hefty chimpanzees and gorillas, our closest relatives, the "dark continent" is home to seventy-two species of primates. This remarkable diversity includes some of the most colorful species, such as the red, blue, and lavender-hued mandrills, the beautifully patterned guenons, and the caped and plume-tailed black-and-white colobus monkeys. Most of Africa's primate species inhabit the sub-Saharan Guinea-Congolian forest block, but a few can be found in drier habitats, including the barbary macaques native to arid North Africa.

Uganda's Kibale Forest in the foothills east of the Ruwenzori Mountains is one of the richest primate-viewing areas in Africa. Here, eleven species find protection in this single reserve. A network of trails through the reserve's equatorial forest makes it possible to observe many, including olive baboons, blue monkeys, red colobus, gray-cheeked mangabeys, even chimpanzees.

However, of the ninety-two countries in the world in which primates live, it is the African nations of Zaire and Cameroon that contain eighteen primate genera each. These numbers are significant, since twenty-one genera inhabit the entire African continent. Zaire provides precious habitat for thirty-seven primate species, Cameroon for thirty-two, making both African countries extremely important in terms of species diversity and primate conservation.

POTTO

(Perodicticus potto)

Pottos are native to the tropical forests of Africa from Guinea, West Africa, to Kenya. At night they move slowly through the canopy, feeding mostly on fruits. They also eat leaves and animal protein in the form of ants, slugs, caterpillars, and beetles. Coarse guard hairs protrude from the back of the neck where the lower cervical vertebrae and the first thoracic vertebrae have been elongated into sub-cutaneous spines that help protect the potto's spinal cord and blood vessels against attacks by predators. Pottos often copulate while hanging by their feet from a branch. A single young is born after a gestation period of about six and a half months. While foraging at night, the mother often parks her infant on a branch for later retrieval.

◁ **The hands of the African potto are specially adapted for gripping tree branches. The index finger has been reduced to a tubercle and the thumb has migrated 180 degrees to face the other digits for more powerful, pincher-like grasping. A claw on the second toe is used for self-grooming.**

◊ **By rubbing urine on their hands and feet, female pottos leave important olfactory messages for all male pottos that follow. Without making contact, a male can monitor a female's reproductive condition so that he's on hand when she is ready to mate.**

▽ **The lesser galago has an active, acrobatic nightlife. Its enormous eyes and large mobile ears are used to scan the dark for insect prey. With elongated lower limbs, strong thigh muscles, and specialized ankle joints, galagos can make vertical leaps of seven feet or more through the trees. Round flat pads on their fingertips enable them to firmly grip the branches.**

LESSER BUSHBABY or
GALAGO

(Galago senegalensis)

Native to Africa, these small, eleven-ounce insectivores are one of the most widespread African primates. They inhabit most forested savanna areas south of the Sahara Desert. The reflective eyeshine of their enormous nocturnal eyes reveals their arboreal location as they leap from branch to branch. Galagos use secretions from glands on their face, chest, arms, elbows, palms, and soles to leave olfactory messages for those that follow. They also "urine wash" as a means of marking and identifying themselves to other galagos. Females can breed twice each year, usually producing twins after a four- to five-month gestation period. The mother carries her young in her mouth for the first two weeks of life, parking them on branches while she feeds almost exclusively on acacia gums and insects.

GREATER BUSHBABY or
THICK-TAILED BUSHBABY

(Otolemur crassicaudatus)

Weighing around four pounds, the greater bushbaby is the largest of the galagos. Unlike its smaller leaping cousins, this nocturnal primate relies more on quadrupedal walking and running to move through the low open forests and woodland savannas of south-central Africa. Twins are typically born in November when food and cover for concealment are most available. Although fruits and gums are their favorite foods, they will also eat slow-moving insects and birds if given the chance.

◊ In contrast to its cautious quadrupedal movement through the trees, the greater bushbaby of Africa can bound like a kangaroo when on the ground, making rapid bipedal leaps.

⌂ The greater or thick-tailed bushbaby of Africa has been killed for its meat and fur and captured for the pet trade. As a result, it is protected by law in South Africa.

GRAY-CHEEKED MANGABEY

(Lophocebus albigena)

Gray-cheeked mangabeys inhabit the primary evergreen forests, disturbed secondary forests, and flooded swamp forests of western Uganda, Kenya, Tanzania, Zaire, and Rwanda. Adult males have laryngeal sacs that they use to produce long, "whoop-gobble" calls. These loud calls are used to maintain distance between groups and identify the animal calling. Gray-cheeked mangabeys also produce baboon-like grunts, staccato barks, and resonating screams. Primarily fruit-eaters, these opportunistic primates raid fields for maize, peanuts, and sweet potatoes. As a result they are killed as pests and hunted for food.

◊ **A gray-cheeked mangabey sits in a tree in Uganda's Kibale National Park. It is here that this species has been most intensely studied by field primatologists.**

CHERRY-CROWNED MANGABEY

(Cercocebus torquatus)

Named for the reddish cap of hair on their heads, these large, slender monkeys can also be identified by the way they carry their tails, held parallel over their backs. Mangabeys fill up their large cheek pouches with fruits, leaves, and insects as they forage during the day. Groups range in size from three to twenty-five individuals or more, and are characterized by a linear hierarchy of adult females. Males leave their natal group when they become sexually mature. The cherry-crowned mangabey is listed as an endangered species throughout its forested range in central West Africa. The species is continuing to decline because of poaching and deforestation.

⬦ **A cherry-crowned mangabey demonstrates its threat posture. Like baboons, mangabeys use their eyes, white eyelids, and canines to embellish facial expressions.**

◊ **A big-eared, pink-skinned infant olive baboon noncha-lantly sprawls over his mother's hands and arms as she enjoys a grooming session with close kin.**

ANUBIS or OLIVE BABOON
(Papio anubis)

Anubis or olive baboons are named after the dark olive-gray color of their coats. Highly adaptable, these 50- to 110-pound primates inhabit the semidesert steppe, arid thorn scrub, open grasslands, plains, savanna, rocky hills, woodlands, and gallery and tropical rain forests of sub-Saharan Africa from Mali to northern Tanzania. Olive baboons communicate with each other using a variety of gestures, facial expressions, and body postures. They also have more than fifteen different vocalizations; many are thought to communicate specific information about their environment—such as, "leopard, watch out!" Troop size varies from eight to one hundred or more members, with larger groups having more than one resident male. Males greet each other in an elaborate ritual of touching and mounting with active facial and vocal signalling. A stable male dominance hierarchy provides structure for the entire troop.

△ **A healthy mother-infant bond is critical for the emotional well-being and ultimate survival of young primates. Here a female olive baboon patiently nurses her playful infant.**

⬆ A bold baboon infant momentarily strolls away from Tranquility Base—its mother. When a baboon troop is on the move, females with infants usually remain in the center of the group, surrounded and protected by the dominant adult males.

▽ Infants routinely attract attention from other troop members. Here a young olive baboon endures a bit of indelicate grooming as his protective mother monitors the encounter.

▽ Two young baboons dine among the thorns of an acacia tree. In addition to eating fruits, leaves, grass, and insects, baboons also eat meat, including young impala, gazelle, bushbuck, and unwary guinea fowl.

◁ A male olive baboon displays his deadly canines. All species of baboons show marked sexual dimorphism in size, weight, and canine length. Not only do males weigh about twice as much as females, but they grow enormous canines, which are used for troop defense and dominance battles.

◁ Robustly built, a male olive baboon helps police and protect his troop in Kenya's Masai Mara National Preserve. Intelligence coupled with brawn, including a mouth full of razor-sharp teeth, makes him a formidable threat.

▷ Yawns carry mixed messages in primate societies. They can be a subtle but effective display of dental weaponry. Among baboons, troop size is often limited by the availability of sleeping sites. Trees provide the best defense against predators; rocky outcrops are preferred next.

⌂ Dominance positions within a baboon troop are determined through social alliances—and aggression. Baboon emotions can quickly flare, as depicted in this high-speed chase across the savanna.

◁ An infant olive baboon clings precariously to the belly of its mother as she tries in vain to outdistance an aggressive male. Her grimace captures the emotional moment in this highly tense, freeze-frame chase.

▽ **A juvenile chacma baboon rides jockey-style on his mother's back near Botswana's Okavango River. The big-eared infant is held in place with back support from the upright base of the mother's tail.**

CHACMA BABOON
(Papio ursinus)

Chacma baboons inhabit the grasslands, woodland savanna, and acacia scrub of southern Africa. They are the most southern-ranging of all baboon species. At birth, infants have conspicuous pink faces and oversized, pink flapping ears. This effect is lost within the first year as they mature. Baboons have been described as "dog-faced," due to their extremely elongated faces. Their long muzzles not only house large canine teeth, but provide a greater surface area for grinding grasses, roots, and tubers with their molars. Small mammals, insects, and birds' eggs are also on the menu, along with crustaceans, which chacma baboons eat along the sea coasts of South Africa. Cheek pouches that open near the lower teeth make it possible for baboons to eat on the run. Should feeding conditions become too competitive, or unsafe, baboons quickly grab and stuff food into their cheek pouches for later dining at leisure.

HAMADRYAS BABOON

(Papio hamadryas)

As true for all species of Old World monkeys, hamadryas baboons rely on a rich repertoire of vocalizations, facial and body gestures, and olfactory and tactile signals to communicate with each other. These signals help an adult male coordinate the activity of his group of females and young, typically numbering up to twelve individuals. Hamadryas have an interesting social structure, made up of varying combinations of one-male units. By day, the units merge to form foraging groups of twenty to seventy individuals. At night, hundreds of baboons may gather to share limited sleeping cliffs.

⇧ **The silver-gray coat and heavy, long-haired shoulder cape distinguish this primate as a male hamadryas baboon. These large quadrupedal primates range from Ethiopia to the extreme southwestern tip of Saudi Arabia. In ancient Egypt, this species was revered as sacred.**

DRILL

(Mandrillus leucophaeus)

Drills are large, forest-dwelling primates native to western Central Africa. They live in one-male and multimale groups that can combine to form large troops of one hundred fifty or more. Male drills are brilliantly colored around the genitals. Here the colors range from bright red, blue, and light purple to lilac and pink. The male's rainbow-hued posterior is said to serve as a beacon when he leads his group single-file through the forest. More likely, their flashy rear ends provide powerful social and sexual signals to females as well as rival males.

▽ In addition to visual signals, male drills communicate with a series of deep grunts and produce a loud, high-pitched "crowing" vocalization used for long-range contact. As if their size and appearance were not intimidating enough, they "threat jerk" toward rivals by abruptly thrusting their heads forward, retracting their eyelids, puckering their lips, and raising the medial crest on their heads.

◊ The black facemask and ears, tufted white beard, and scarlet lower lip identify this primate as a male drill. The massive muzzle with prominent bony swellings on either side of the nose also indicates that this is a male. Not only do their skulls show marked sexual dimorphism, but so do their canines. This endangered species is native to the rain and riverine forests of western Central Africa, specifically Cameroon, southeast Nigeria, and the island of Bioko, once known as Fernando Póo.

◊ The largest of all monkeys, mandrills are a forested version of Africa's terrestrial baboons. Here, a brightly colored male shows off the massive muzzle, grooved blue nasal swellings, and barn-red nose characteristic of the species.

MANDRILL

(Mandrillus sphinx)

Mandrills are forest dwellers that inhabit the dense, primary rain forests of Cameroon, Equatorial Guinea, Gabon, and the Congo. The females and young climb into the trees to feed while the males spend most of their time on the ground. The male genitals are brightly colored—violet, red, and blue. These same hues appear on their faces, framed with yellow-orange beards and whiskers. Mandrills live in one-male units that occasionally aggregate into larger herds. The vivid colors both fore and aft help the males coordinate group movement.

△ A male mandrill exposes his food- and battle-worn teeth, including his huge canines. The one in his lower left jaw has been broken.

△ A young mandrill keeps in stride with its mother. Coloration of the females and young is much less dramatic than in the adult males.

GELADA

(Theropithecus gelada)

Geladas are dramatic primates. Sexual dimorphism is most pronounced in this species—in size, weight, canine development, and the shape and size of the bare skin patches exposed on their chests. When in heat, the females' pink, hourglass-shaped chest patches become swollen and fluid-filled, signaling her readiness to mate. Only the males sport long, heavy manes that flow over their shoulders. These are tossed about during aggressive displays, which also include ground-slapping threats, white eyelid flashes, and the species' famous facial grimace—the "lip flip"—when the upper lip is flipped back to reveal the white teeth and gums of the upper jaw. Geladas inhabit the montane grasslands of the high, treeless plateau between the deep gorges of northern and central Ethiopia. Here they live in one-male groups of up to twenty individuals that congregate into larger foraging parties by day when food is plentiful. To avoid predators, geladas also congregate into larger herds at night to sleep along the steep cliffs of the gorges. As many as four hundred geladas have been counted in such sleeping groups.

⇧ Typical of ground-dwelling primates, geladas show striking sexual dimorphism and can form large groups, depending on available resources. The males use dramatic facial displays to intimidate other geladas, including white eyelid flashes and rapid "lip flips" of the upper lip to reveal their white gums, teeth, and large canines.

◁ The blue scrotum and red penis against white inner thighs identifies this primate as a male vervet monkey. Adult males use their colorful genitalia during "red, white, and blue" dominance displays.

VERVET MONKEY

(Cercopithecus aethiops johnstoni)

Vervet monkeys are probably one of the most familiar, and most studied, species of African guenons, because they are so abundant and widespread. Only the availability of sleeping trees and water seems to affect their distribution. Vervets easily adapt to human intrusion. They differ from the other guenon species by being the smallest and most terrestrial. These opportunistic omnivores forage primarily for fruits and seeds, but will also eat flowers, eggs, baby birds, and lizards. In parts of West Africa, the vervet monkey is considered a delicacy.

◁ Ready for mischief, two young vervet monkeys perch in the afternoon sun at Amboseli National Park. Vervet monkeys use separate alarm calls for different kinds of predators, such as eagles, pythons, and leopards. Crowned and martial eagles as well as leopards frequently prey on these active, vocal monkeys.

◁ Two young vervet monkeys in Kenya's Amboseli National Park perform acrobatics on a tree branch. As true for the young of all highly intelligent animals, play behavior helps perfect the social and physical skills required in adulthood.

SCHMIDT'S or RED-TAILED MONKEY

(Cercopithecus ascanius)

Named for its copper-red tail, this African guenon is one of five subspecies. Heart-shaped white facial hair around the nose gives these plant-eating monkeys a flat-nosed appearance. Unlike other guenons, the males do not produce the characteristic "boom" calls. One-male groups are the most common social organization. While some groups never have more than one male, others may have three or more during an influx of extra group males. Because the males come and go, females with their young form the permanent core of the group. The adult females even defend their territories.

△ **Two red-tailed or Schmidt's monkeys rest in a tree in Uganda's Kibale National Park. Cheek pouches enable guenons to feed rapidly and then retire to safety to chew and swallow their food at leisure.**

DIANA MONKEY

(Cercopithecus diana)

Cheek pouches are well-developed in all guenons, including the Diana monkey of West Africa. This beautifully marked primate uses its tail to balance as it leaps through the trees. Diana monkeys differ from other guenons by their black faces with white ruff and beard and the white stripe that runs down each thigh. Group size ranges from fourteen to fifty individuals. During the day they feed on fruit, seeds, leaves, and arthropods. Diana monkeys are protected in three national parks and three forest reserves of Africa.

▽ A Diana monkey, native to the forests of West Africa, displays its colorful coat. Apparently, it is a coat to die for, as many of these monkeys have been killed for their striking pelts.

△ Forest vegetation makes it difficult to observe guenons in the wild. As a result, little more than half of the species have been studied. A Diana monkey photographed in West Africa illustrates the point.

HAMLYN'S OWL-FACED MONKEY

(Cercopithecus hamlyni)

Guenons are the most common monkeys of Africa, of which there are at least twenty different species. Although similar in body build, their coat color is extremely variable. The distinctive white nose stripe and bright blue genitals help distinguish Hamlyn's owl-faced monkey from other species. This semiterrestrial primate ranges from eastern Zaire to southwestern Uganda in lowland, bamboo, and montane forests at elevations up to 12,000 feet or more. Adult males produce audible "boom" calls that carry great distances through the forest.

◊ **The white brow-to-lip racing stripe and owl-like ruff of fur encircling the head identify this monkey as a Hamlyn's owl-faced guenon, native to the forests of Zaire and Uganda.**

L'HOEST MONKEY

(Cercopithecus lhoesti)

When chased by people, this African monkey flees on the ground, making it one of the more terrestrial of the African guenons. It also has one of the broadest muzzles, which turns bright violet in the adult male. Group size varies from five to twenty-five individuals, depending on available resources. Because the average group tenure for any adult male lasts only about three months, competition among males is intense for such coveted breeding positions. Humans are the most serious threat to the L'Hoest monkey, because of habitat destruction and hunting for its pelt and meat.

⌂ **A blue monkey rests in a tree near Lake Manyara, Tanzania. Found from Ethiopia to Zambia, blue monkeys have the widest distribution of all cercopithecine primates.**

BLUE MONKEY

(Cercopithecus mitis)

Most guenons, such as the blue monkey, inhabit the forests of West and Central Africa. However, of all the guenon species, it is the blue monkey that occupies the most diverse habitats, including primary forest, montane bamboo forest, coastal scrub, and dry woodland. Primarily arboreal, blue monkeys are quick and agile in the trees. Female preference drives blue monkey reproduction. When receptive, females solicit males through conspicuous postures and facial expressions. A single offspring is produced following a five- to six-month gestation period.

⌂ **The semiterrestrial L'Hoest monkey, photographed here in Uganda's Kibale National Park, is one of more than twenty species of guenons native to the forests of Africa. It frequently spends time in the lower canopy, fifteen feet or more from the ground.**

▽ Known for its colorful face, the De Brazza's monkey is one of the largest and most sexually dimorphic of the cerco-pithecines. Males average fourteen pounds, females only eight. Like other species of guenons, De Brazza's monkeys share the trait of age color changes, as this upside-down orange infant shows.

DE BRAZZA'S MONKEY

(Cercopithecus neglectus)

The bright orange crest of fur above the eyebrow ridges and white beard identify this species as a De Brazza's monkey. These arboreal primates prefer dense vegetation near streams and rivers in East and Central Africa. Unafraid of water, they do not hesitate to leap into a stream if it needs to be crossed. In addition to facial displays, auditory vocalizations, and body posturing, De Brazza's monkeys use secretions from their sternal glands to communicate with each other. Grooming also plays an important role in group cohesion and maintenance of social relationships among kin.

▽ **A male patas monkey plays with a youngster. When water is available, patas monkeys drink regularly. When it is not, these desert-adapted primates survive by using the moisture from their food.**

PATAS MONKEY

(Erythrocebus patas)

Patas monkeys inhabit the open woodlands and savanna of West and East Africa. Thanks to their cheetah-like gait, they hold the record for being the fastest of the terrestrial primates. By rising up on their digits, they can run up to fifty kilometers an hour. Sexually dimorphic in size and weight, males weigh twenty-four pounds, females half that. Females synchronize their reproductive cycles so that most infants are born during the dry season between December and January. By the time the youngsters are old enough to wean at four to five months of age, the wet season vegetation is most abundant. Males produce alarm barks to warn of cat predators; females and juveniles give high-pitched chirps. For greater protection from predators at night, these ground-dwelling primates sleep in trees.

RED COLOBUS

(Procolobus badius tephrosceles)

Red colobus monkeys forage for leaves in the tropical rain forests and gallery forests of East and Central Africa. Aside from eating, colobus spend a great deal of their day doing nothing. This inactivity is thought to be the result of their specialized digestive system, since fermentation of plant material is a slow process. Multimale red colobus groups as large as eighty individuals have been recorded. Infanticide by adult males does occur. In the Kibale Forest of western Uganda, red colobus share the same habitat with black-and-white colobus. This is possible because the two species do not compete for similar foods.

⬑ **Perched high in a tree of Uganda's Kibale Forest, a red colobus monkey feeds on a branchful of leaves. Lacking thumbs for opposable grasping, colobus monkeys simply use a hook-grip to pull the leaves to their mouths.**

◊ A group of black-and-white colobus monkeys *(C. guereza occidentalis)* takes a feeding break high in a tree in Uganda's Kibale Forest. To process their diet of bulky plant material, colobus's stomachs are enlarged and divided into compartments. This gives most leaf-eating monkeys a rather potbellied appearance.

ABYSSINIAN BLACK-AND-WHITE COLOBUS

(Colobus guereza occidentalis)

ANGOLAN BLACK-AND-WHITE COLOBUS

(Colobus angolensis angolensis)

Colobus monkeys are the largest of the African colobines, or leaf-eating monkeys. These boldly marked arboreal primates have beautiful plume-like tails that measure one and a third times their head and body length. Reduced thumbs and unusually long fingers make it possible for colobus to use their arms to swing through the trees in search of food. They eat fruit, young and old leaves, flowers, and twigs. Their large four-chambered stomachs digest plant cellulose through bacterial fermentation. To expel the methane and carbon dioxide produced as a byproduct, colobus often belch in each other's faces as a friendly social gesture. Their specialized digestive system enables them to eat leaf diets that other primates can't.

▽ The social organization of colobus monkeys consists of a single adult male with several females and their young. Black-and-white colobus infants are born pure white. However, not all survive: cases of infanticide have been documented when a new male takes over a group of females with young. *(C. guereza occidentalis)*

▽ The flowing white mantle and long white-tipped tails of the black-and-white colobus monkeys *(C. angolensis angolensis)* stand out in sharp contrast to East Africa's green forests. Their dramatic coats serve as visual signals not only to each other, but also to poachers who profit from the illegal sale of their exotic pelts.

◁ A black-and-white colobus monkey *(C. guereza occidentalis)* photographed at Kenya's Lake Nakuru shows off its namesake markings. Most of their preferred food—leaves with some fruit and flowers—grows in the forest canopy.

◊ **A female bonobo holds her infant close. Reduced male aggression, strong affiliative bonds between males and females, and frequent sex characterize bonobo society. These rare apes are found only in Zaire, in the forests south of the Lualaba and Zaire rivers.**

BONOBO or PYGMY CHIMPANZEE
(Pan paniscus)

One of two species of chimpanzees, the bonobo or pygmy chimpanzee inhabits a restricted area of tropical rain forest in Zaire. It differs from the more abundant chimpanzee *(Pan troglodytes)* not so much in size but by having a more rounded head, lighter build, and relatively longer legs. Bonobos also seem to be more acrobatic, jumping from tree to tree. Like all apes, they have no tails. The only apparent sexual dimorphism is in their canines—even community ranges are shared equally between the sexes. Their reproductive history explains why bonobos are vulnerable. Females first give birth at age twelve or thirteen. Subsequent births then occur every five to five and a half years after each offspring is weaned at around four to five years of age. Even after weaning, the young remain emotionally dependent on the mother for several more years.

The Bonobo Protection Fund was founded in 1990 to protect the bonobo while educating the people of Zaire about the importance of their conservation. Bonobos are hunted as food, killed to produce charms and trinkets, and sold to an illegal pet trade. Accelerating habitat loss also threatens their future.

For those who still dispute our relationship to nonhuman primates, the A antigen of the bonobo or pygmy chimpanzee *(Pan paniscus)* is indistinguishable from the A1 antigen of *Homo sapiens.*

◊ **A female bonobo lounges in simian repose. Communication between bonobos is varied. They use sounds, body gestures, facial grimaces, and sexual gestures to convey mood and intent. Because they freely use their hands to gesture, bonobos have been used in laboratory studies of sign language.**

◊ **Grooming is a social activity that helps reinforce the bonds between primates. Here, a group of chimpanzees in Tanzania's Mahale National Park line up for a session.**

CHIMPANZEE

(Pan troglodytes)

Classified as a great ape, the chimpanzee of West, Central, and East Africa is a large primate, with males weighing nearly one hundred and fifty pounds. Chimp society is dominated by the adult males. In fact, male kin groups define territory. Their aggressive raids on neighboring chimp communities can be deadly. Chimps arm-swing and climb through trees. On the ground they move bipedally as well as knuckle-walk. The sounds produced by chimpanzees are complex, reflecting both their intelligence and sophisticated social organization. They bark, squeak, grunt, pant, laugh, and scream. In addition to fruit, leaves, and other vegetarian fare, male chimpanzees join together and stalk and hunt small antelope, pigs, baboons, and monkeys, particularly red colobus. The meat is often shared.

Female chimpanzees mate with a variety of males during their period of genital swelling. However, as each female approaches ovulation, the high-ranking males compete for access. Aggression plays an important role in structuring chimpanzee society.

◊ **Chimpanzees** *(Pan troglodytes)* **are native to West, Central, and East Africa, where they inhabit both forests and woodland savannas dominated by grassland. Here a chimp feeds on the leaves of a fig tree in Mahale National Park, Tanzania.**

◁ Partly arboreal and partly terrestrial, chimpanzees nest in trees at night and feed in fruit trees by day. Most of their travel, however, is done on the ground. Recent logging activity in the tropical forests of Gabon has triggered savage territorial wars between chimpanzee groups. It is estimated that the chimpanzee population has been reduced from fifty thousand to thirty thousand since logging operations have begun.

△ The toughened fingers of a chimpanzee *(Pan troglodytes)* tell of the wear and tear this hand has experienced during a lifetime of foraging for plant material.

▽ A white goatee and rump patch identify this primate gymnast as a young chimpanzee. Like human children, infant chimps crave affection and spend a considerable amount of time at play.

△ Strong family ties characterize chimpanzee society, as do empathetic relationships among kin. Should a young chimpanzee become orphaned, older siblings, including brothers, will often care for and protect their motherless kin.

▽ Although the young are weaned at around five years of age, a close bond with the mother remains. Chimpanzee offspring as old as eight years have died if orphaned.

◊ To look into the eyes of a chimpanzee is to look into the eyes of a human. There is no denying their keen intelligence. Begun in 1960, Jane Goodall's ongoing study of chimpanzees at Tanzania's Gombe National Park is the longest field study of any animal in the world. Her long-term research, spanning nearly four decades, has revealed that these smart apes make and use tools, hunt in organized groups, eat meat, self-medicate with medicinal plants, and occasionally engage in intergroup warfare. Such knowledge underscores the need to increase conservation efforts on behalf of wild chimpanzees and their native habitats, as well as to provide far more humane conditions for those held in captivity.

◊ **Gorillas are the largest living primates, yet they remained unknown to science until 1847. Here, a male western lowland gorilla displays his inherent dominance. Researchers think that nearly half of the existing population of western lowland gorillas inhabits Gabon where vast tracks of forest still exist.**

WESTERN LOWLAND GORILLA

(Gorilla gorilla gorilla)

Gorillas are currently classified with *Homo sapiens* in the family Hominidae. Humans and apes diverged during the Miocene era about six to ten million years ago. Three subspecies of gorillas are now recognized, the western lowland gorilla, the eastern lowland gorilla, and the mountain gorilla. They are distinguished from each other by length of body hair, variation in coat color, and the size of their jaws and teeth.

The eastern lowland gorilla *(G. g. graueri)* inhabits a small area of forest from eastern Zaire to the west of Lake Tanganyika. Like the mountain gorilla, this subspecies has a black coat but with shorter hair. Because of its reduced numbers and limited range, this subspecies is listed as endangered by the World Conservation Union (IUCN).

The western lowland gorilla is not only the smallest and least endangered of the three subspecies, but it has the widest distribution. This subspecies lives in a variety of forest habitats in the Congo, Gabon, Equatorial Guinea, Cameroon, the Central African Republic, Nigeria, and Zaire. Gorillas are primarily vegetarians, eating fruit, leaves, and plant parts. Male western lowland gorillas weigh around 300 pounds while the sexually dimorphic females weigh half as much. When standing, an adult male can reach a height of five feet six inches. Because of their size, gorillas are almost completely terrestrial. At night they sleep mostly on the ground, sometimes in trees, on cushioned nests they construct with branches and leaves.

◊ **Much can be learned about the importance of healthy mother-infant bonds by studying primates, particularly the great apes. Here a foraging female gorilla provides a warm, secure surface for her dozing infant.**

◊ An infant lowland gorilla tentatively explores its surroundings. If female, she will have to mature for eight years before she can reproduce. Gorillas are vulnerable to extinction because of their slow reproductive rate. In a typical twenty-five-year period of fertility, an adult female will produce only three offspring that survive to breeding age.

◊ This two-month-old western lowland gorilla, born in captivity at Seattle's Woodland Park Zoo, shows one of the distinctive physical features that differentiates lowland gorillas from mountain gorillas: Its nose has a continuous, heart-shaped ridge all around the nostrils.

⬦ Despite all that we have learned about primate intelligence and social structure, people continue to harm these remarkable animals. Gorilla meat is occasionally sold in the meat markets and restaurants in Cameroon, Gabon, and the Congo Republic. Gorilla body parts are still offered illegally to tourists as souvenir trinkets and wildlife trophies.

⌃ **Almost entirely ground-dwelling, gorillas prefer open-canopy forests that allow light to reach the forest floor. Here a male mountain gorilla feeds on Rwanda's lush vegetation. Unlike chimpanzees, wild mountain gorillas have never been observed using tools to "fish" for termites. Instead, their diet includes roots, stems, leaves, vines, fruits, flowers, and bamboo.**

MOUNTAIN GORILLA

(Gorilla gorilla beringei)

Mountain gorillas are the rarest of the three subspecies of gorillas, found only in the Virunga mountains of southwest Uganda, northwest Rwanda, and eastern Zaire. This subspecies has the largest jaws and teeth of the three, and the longest black hair. Adult males can weigh four hundred pounds or more and stand six feet tall. Most of our knowledge about the ecology and social behavior of all gorillas comes from studies of this subspecies. At the Karisoke Research Center in Rwanda, Dian Fossey began her field observations of wild mountain gorillas in 1968. Ongoing studies of several groups at Karisoke still continue as they have for nearly thirty years. Disease, civil war, poaching, and continued habitat loss have left this subspecies vulnerable to extinction. Only about six hundred mountain gorillas remain in the wild.

◊ Infant gorillas are vulnerable to attack from unrelated males. During a fifteen-year research period in Rwanda, infanticide was the cause of 38 percent of infant deaths.

▽ A female mountain gorilla cradles her offspring in the rain at Rwanda's Virunga Volcanoes National Park.

◊ Among gorillas, male protection is essential to female reproductive success, so it is in a female's best interest to choose a quality male partner. Transfer patterns of female gorillas between groups indicate that they actively choose their breeding partners, who are usually the older, more experienced silverback males.

◊ More than fifteen distinct gorilla vocalizations have been identified, including pant-grunts, barks, and high-pitched screeches. Such a rich vocal repertoire reflects the complexity of gorilla social structure, first documented by the late Dian Fossey.

◊ When a male gorilla hoots, then growls, then puts a leaf between his lips—watch out! Next he will rise to his full bipedal height of nearly six feet, beat his bare chest with cupped hands to produce the characteristic "pok-pok-pok" sound—then charge.

⬠ A male mountain gorilla peers through the vegetation at Uganda's Bwindi Impenetrable Forest, his size and strength concealed behind a cover of delicate leaves. Gorillas are sexually dimorphic. Males can weigh twice as much as females. By the age of eleven, young males reach sexual maturity and begin to dominate most females during aggressive interactions.

The lush tropical rain forests of south and Southeast Asia contain thirteen primate genera and seventy-one different species—a handful of which live in temperate Asia. From the big-eyed nocturnal tarsiers and the slow-moving lorises to the high-speed, brachiating gibbons that swing from tree to tree, Asia is home to some of the most amazing—and some of the most endangered—primates.

Thirty-six species live in Indonesia alone, of which nineteen are endemic (found nowhere else in the world). Among them are the yellow-banded leaf monkeys native to Sumatra, the proboscis monkeys, and the orangutans, the only reddish-colored great ape in existence. Indonesia is thus a particularly high-priority area for global primate conservation.

SLENDER LORIS

(Loris tardigradus)

The slender loris inhabits the forests and woodlands of southern India and Sri Lanka. Described as a banana on stilts, this small, solitary, tail-less prosimian uses its stilt-like legs to navigate tree branches at night with slow deliberate movement. Extremely flexible hips and spine enable it to sleep curled up in a ball by day and to maneuver with grace and stealth through dense forests at night. Slender loris rely on olfactory signals to communicate with each other: They transfer urine to their hands and feet to leave scent trails over the branches.

◊ **An infant slender loris holds its mother tight as she moves at night through a forest in Sri Lanka. Lorises' big eyes and ears enable them to search for insects in the dark.**

SLOW LORIS

(Nycticebus coucang)

The slow loris of Southeast Asia does not leap through the trees as other primates do. Instead, it uses its feet like clamps to move methodically hand over hand through the canopy. Lorises can maintain their grasp on branches for hours at a time because their hands are served by a specialized capillary network that other primates lack. They have stumps for tails and eyes that are "fixed," which means they must move their head to change focus. As if habitat loss were not threatening enough, slow lorises are hunted for their eyes. They are collected as love charms and for use in Asian medicine.

▽ **The slow loris is a prosimian native to the rain forests of Southeast Asia. Active only at night, this quiet little primate is difficult to see in the wild. It feeds on leaves, fruit, birds' eggs, baby birds, and insects.**

△ **A slow loris makes a head-first, vertical descent in a forest of Southeast Asia. Reduced second digits enable the hands and feet to operate like pincers as they slowly but tightly grip and release each tree branch.**

HORSFIELD'S TARSIER
(Tarsius bancanus)

The enormous eyes of a Horsfield's tarsier dominate its tiny face. To compensate for their immobility, tarsiers can turn their heads in owl-like fashion nearly 180 degrees in each direction. The tarsier gets its name from its elongated tarsal bones, which are used to propel the little primate through the canopy. As a further adaptation for powerful leaping, the tibia and fibula of each leg are fused along the lower third of their length. Flat, fleshy pads at the end of each digit help these acrobatic leapers to grip smooth vertical surfaces. Horsfield's tarsiers live in the forests of Borneo, Java, Sumatra, and the adjacent islands. Unique among primates, tarsiers are exclusively predators, fueled by a diet of animal protein. In addition to insects, Horsfield's tarsiers also stalk birds, snakes, and lizards, usually eating them head first.

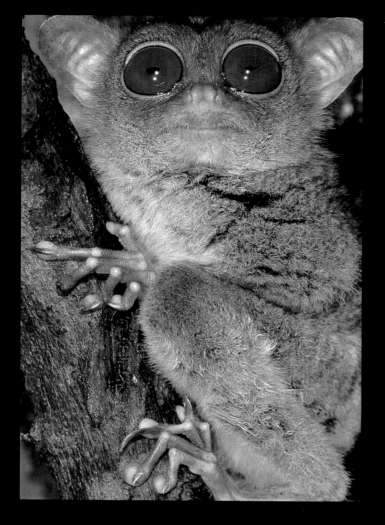

PHILIPPINE TARSIER

(Tarsius syrichta)

Philippine tarsiers live in both primary (unlogged) and secondary (disturbed) tropical forests. They form social groups of two to six animals consisting of a mated pair and their offspring. Vocal communication in this species is elaborate. Family members sleep together by day, and remain close to each other while foraging. Philippine tarsiers have enormous eyes and large, mobile ears for nocturnal pursuit of lizards and insects. To prevent injury during predatory attacks and movement through the dense understory (trees of the lower canopy), their ears can be folded close to their heads. These small vertical clingers and leapers are named for the elongated tarsal bones that aid their locomotion. When threatened, Philippine tarsiers can make tremendous leaps of eighteen feet or more.

⌂ A Philippine tarsier from Southeast Asia shows off the anatomy that makes it possible to hunt for insects and lizards at night—big eyes and ears. Flat pads at the end of most digits enable this small primate to grip tree trunks when it leaps. Specialized grooming claws are located on the second and third digits of each foot.

◊ This big-eyed little creature is not an alien but a Horsfield's tarsier, native to Borneo, Java, and Sumatra. These nocturnal prosimians are built to vertically cling and leap through the forest, and pounce on insect and reptilian prey they spot on the ground.

LONG-TAILED or
CRAB-EATING MACAQUE
(Macaca fascicularis)

The long-tailed or crab-eating macaques are native to the rain forests of Southeast Asia. They are named for their long graceful tails, which touch the ground when they walk, and their habit of feeding on crabs and shellfish in mangrove swamps. This highly adaptable species prefers primary riverine or coastal forests, but can live just as easily in disturbed habitats. In many cases, human habitat alterations have benefited this species by providing additional food sources, such as rice, cassava leaves, and taro plants. In addition to alarm calls, loud screeches, and shrieks, long-tailed macaques use an animated repertoire of facial gestures to communicate with each other, some of which are quite subtle.

▷ **A long-tailed macaque has a close encounter with a tourist in Borneo. Because primates are unpredictable, such close contact is not a good idea.**

◁ **An infant long-tailed macaque is held close by its mother in a rain forest canopy of Thailand. The mother-infant bond is critical to the survival and development of a young primate.**

PIG-TAILED MACAQUE

(Macaca nemestrina)

Pig-tailed macaques are forest monkeys native to the primary and second-growth forests of Southeast Asia. Their short tails, long faces, and thick whorling cap of short dark hair identify them. Like many species of macaques, pig-tails use their light-colored eyelids to accentuate facial gestures, including threatening stares, pout faces, and fear grimaces. Pig-tails live in multimale groups that subdivide to forage in the lower canopy and on the forest floor. Compared to other species of macaques, pig-tails tend to be fairly quiet. Researchers think this is an adaptation that helps them avoid terrestrial predators.

△ **A female pig-tailed macaque forages for food on the floor of a tropical forest in Southeast Asia. Old World monkeys, particularly the mandrills, baboons, geladas, and macaques, are second only to man in the use of their opposable thumbs and fingertips for precise manipulation of small objects.**

◁ **A long-tailed or crab-eating macaque hitches a ride on the rump of a deer in Thailand. These versatile primates live in a variety of habitats but prefer forests close to water. Although tree-dwelling, they readily come to the ground to raid cultivated areas and loiter around temples and botanical gardens.**

SULAWESI CRESTED MACAQUE

(Macaca nigra)

Formerly known as Celebes macaques, these all-black primates recently underwent a name change when the islands on which they live were renamed the Sulawesi Islands. Inaccurately referred to as "apes" because they are jet black and tail-less, these large primates are Old World monkeys, not apes. Sulawesi crested macaques "lip smack" to show aggression and can produce a "high grin" by pulling their upper lips back so only their teeth are visible. In lieu of pale eyelids to flash during visual displays, this species moves their scalps to raise and lower their pronounced head crests.

⌂ **A male Sulawesi crested macaque threatens by flashing his large canines. His bright red scrotum is visible, as are his big toes, which he uses to grab the ankles of females during copulation.**

◊ **Lion-tailed macaques live in social groups that are organized around the lifelong bonds formed between mothers and daughters.**

◊ Lion-tailed macaques are native to southern India, where they are endangered. They are considered the most arboreal of all macaque species.

LION-TAILED MACAQUE

(Macaca silenus)

Several obvious lion-like features have given this macaque its common name: A large ruff of golden-gray fur surrounds their all-black faces, and their long tails are tufted at the end. These elegant-looking fruit-eaters prefer primary forests, where they form multimale groups of twelve to thirty animals. The bonds between mothers and daughters continue throughout their lives, forming the basis for group stability and structure. Lion-tailed macaques are highly endangered. They are restricted to a narrow belt of evergreen and semievergreen monsoon forests in the western Ghats mountains of southern India.

⬡ **A group of Japanese macaques pass a cold winter day by soaking in warm thermal waters. During winter food shortages, they survive by eating tree bark.**

⬡ **Grooming helps maintain the intricate social bonds between primates. Grooming partners reflect not only kinship lines, but the group's dominance hierarchy. Here, a Japanese macaque enjoys a hands-on session.**

JAPANESE MACAQUE or
SNOW MONKEY

(Macaca fuscata fuscata)

Except for *Homo sapiens*, macaques are the most wide-ranging genus of primates. They occur from northern Africa, across the Indian sub-continent, and throughout Southeast Asia. Japanese macaques are part of this remarkable radiation, living on Japan's Honshu, Shikoku, Kyushu, and Yakushima islands. These robustly built monkeys live in social groups that are based on lifelong kinship hierarchies between mothers and daughters. Female choice regulates mating. Macaques combine body language, facial gestures, and vocalizations to communicate information about food, mood, danger, social rank, and sex. Stuffing their cheek pouches with food, Japanese macaques eat everything from leaves, fruit, and berries to insects, small animals—and crops. Snow monkeys have been officially protected in Japan since 1947.

◌ **A female Japanese macaque cuddles her infant. Their dense fur can range in color from brown to nearly white.**

◁ **Protected by his thick brown fur, a young Japanese macaque huddles in the snow. His bare pink face will eventually turn red as he matures.**

◇ **A female Japanese macaque takes time-out on a rock. Like a person, her wrinkled red face and contemplative expression show the wear of time.**

▷ **Two young Japanese macaques use their expressive faces to show concern. Their bare faces, mobile lips, dramatic eyes, and body posture are used to successfully convey information about their moods and environment.**

GOLDEN or SNUB-NOSED LANGUR

(Rhinopithecus roxellana)

The golden monkey or snub-nosed langur inhabits the bamboo jungles, coniferous forests, and rhododendron thickets found in the high mountains of central and western China. This area is snowbound in the winter. To adapt to the cold, golden monkeys have developed robust bodies and long thick fur, particularly over their shoulders. During winter they survive by eating slow-growing lichens. The golden monkey's upturned nose and bright blue face are offset by flame-orange fur. Sexual dimorphism is expressed in the greater length of the males' canines. The males also produce wart-like growths at the corners of their upper lips, which are considered a secondary sexual trait.

◊ **The fire-orange fur of the snub-nosed langur, or golden monkey, has been its undoing. The monkeys are killed for their beautiful pelts and also their bones, which are believed by Asians to hold special medicinal powers.**

DOUC LANGUR

(Pygathrix nemaeus)

The Douc langur is a large, endangered primate native to the rain forests of Laos and Vietnam. With almond-shaped eyes and white whiskers and beard, these colorful monkeys are visually dramatic—even more so when they hold their arms outstretched above their heads to make spectacular fifteen- to eighteen-foot leaps from tree to tree. Bombing and the use of defoliants during the Vietnam War destroyed large areas of their arboreal habitat.

◊ **Douc langurs, native to Indochina, are agile, tree-dwelling vegetarians. They eat primarily young leaves, fruits, and flowers, from which they obtain adequate protein and fluids.**

◊ **Douc langurs live in one-male or multi-male groups that range in size from three to eleven individuals. Black-faced infants are born following a gestation period of about five and a half months. In the first days of life, females other than the mother also handle and groom the infant.**

▷ Found in the forests of Indochina, the Douc langur is a large monkey that shows no sexual dimorphism in size, and very little in coloration. Primarily arboreal, this colorful primate makes frequent, spectacular leaps between trees.

◁ An artist would be hard-pressed to create a more colorful primate than the Douc langur. Its human-like face, encircled with white whiskers and beard, gray pot-bellied stomach, white forearms, bright red legs, and black hands and feet make it appear as if it were dressed in costume.

PROBOSCIS MONKEY

(Nasalis larvatus)

Proboscis monkeys live primarily in the mangrove swamps of Borneo, along the estuaries and tidal creeks. Populations also extend along rivers into areas of lowland rain forest farther inland. Proboscis monkeys are large primates. Males weigh around forty-four pounds, females roughly half that. They move quadrupedally through the trees, making acrobatic leaps with arms and legs outstretched. Proboscis monkeys live in multimale groups of twenty or more individuals. When threatened, adult males face the source of danger and begin to "honk" loudly. With each vocalization, their noses slightly inflate and stiffen. They also growl and shriek, and make distinctive braying calls in the morning and evening. Proboscis monkeys are endangered; more than half of their mangrove habitats have been destroyed by human encroachment.

▷ **A male proboscis monkey makes a high-flying leap from one canopy to another in a Borneo forest. Should a deep-water channel separate a proboscis monkey from access to a desired tree, it will descend from the canopy and swim across. Slight webbing between their digits helps make this possible.**

◊ A female proboscis monkey tenderly cradles her youngster. At birth, the infant's hair is almost black, its face deep blue. By three months of age, the facial pigmentation turns gray as the birth coat brightens to the adult orange.

◊ Male proboscis monkeys have extremely large, pendulous noses that hang below their mouths. The bulbous structure may help to resonate the male's loud vocalizations. Such obvious sexual dimorphism makes it easy to tell the genders apart.

⬦ A female proboscis monkey intently grooms another female who is holding an infant. This intimate glimpse into the lives of two proboscis monkeys shows how important grooming behavior is to the social bonds between primates.

BANDED LEAF MONKEY

(Presbytis melalophos)

Banded leaf monkeys inhabit the tropical rain forests of Malaysia, Sumatra, Java, and Borneo. Adults vary in color from gray, black, or red to brown, depending on geographic location. In contrast, the infants are born all white with a dark stripe running down their backs to the tips of their tails. Leaf monkeys leap and swing through the canopy in pursuit of a folivorous diet. With arms outstretched above their heads, they catapult from tree crown to tree crown. Enlarged salivary glands and a sacculated stomach aid in the fermentation of their bulky plant foods.

⌂ **Banded leaf monkeys inhabit the tropical forests of Malaysia and Indonesia. The sound of their leaping, branch-crashing movements through the trees is often the first indication of their presence.**

YELLOW BANDED LEAF MONKEY

(Presbytis melalophos fluviatilis)

◊ **This visually striking primate is a subspecies of banded leaf monkey, native to the tropical forests of Sumatra. The Latin name *fluviatilis* refers to its beautiful yellow coloration.**

JAVAN BLACK LEAF MONKEY

(Trachypithecus auratus)

The Javan leaf monkey is an endangered species that lives in the tropical rain forests of Indonesia. While its fur is normally black, a golden phase also occurs. Both sexes weigh about fourteen pounds. Females give birth to a single infant following a six- to seven-month gestation period. The infant nurses well into its second year before weaning. Like other leaf monkeys, males make loud calls, which are thought to help maintain intergroup spacing. All leaf monkeys have long tails, which fly out behind them as they make spectacular leaps from tree to tree. Group size ranges from three to twenty monkeys. In Indonesia, the species is protected in the Gunung Halimun Reserve, which contains the largest area of primary rain forest left in Java.

⬖ A female Javan leaf monkey (pictured here during the golden phase) holds her infant close. As for most primate species, habitat loss has taken its toll on these animals.

SILVERED LEAF MONKEY

(Trachypithecus cristatus)

The silvered leaf monkey's shaggy, silvered hair and highly conspicuous, bright-orange infants make this species easy to recognize. Native to Southeast Asia, these leaf-eating primates inhabit a variety of forest types. With visibility restricted in the forest canopy, the sounds they make not only help promote group cohesion, but play an important role in territorial defense. Made day and night, their loud calls serve as location markers. When territorial disputes do arise, they can be prolonged and noisy. Much is at stake, as infanticide sometimes happens after a male takeover occurs. In parts of their range, silvered leaf monkeys are still hunted as a source of meat and medicine.

⬀ **Silvered leaf monkeys inhabit the forests of Southeast Asia, where they are virtually surrounded by food. While their diet consists mostly of young and mature leaves, they also eat fruit, flowers, buds, seeds, and bark.**

◊ **Infant silvered leaf monkeys are bright orange at birth. By three months of age, their hair begins to change color until, at six months, it matches the dark gray of the adults.**

SPECTACLED or DUSKY LEAF MONKEY

(Trachypithecus obscurus)

FRANÇOIS' LEAF MONKEY

(Trachypithecus francoisi)

François' leaf monkeys inhabit mountainous monsoon forests from central Laos and Vietnam to southeastern China. These Old World primates are black with white cheeks. A large black crest peaks at the top of their heads. Carrying great distances through the forest and echoing off the mountainsides, their loud calls sound throughout the day. François' leaf monkeys were reduced by the bombing and defoliation during the Vietnam War. Though they are listed as endangered, some hunting of this species continues—for the unsubstantiated medicinal properties of their carpal bones.

Dusky or spectacled leaf monkeys are named for the white ring of skin around their eyes. A patch of white hair over their lips and chin also stands out against their otherwise black faces. They, too, produce infants that are covered with bright orange hair at birth. Spectacled leaf monkeys inhabit both primary and secondary forests in Southeast Asia. In addition to leaves, they also eat fruits and flowers, and will invade cultivated areas to feed on rubber trees, bamboo, citrus, and jackfruit.

◊ **The spectacled or dusky leaf monkey inhabits the tropical rain forests of the Malay peninsula, including parts of Burma and Thailand.**

◊ **François' leaf monkeys are endangered throughout their range in Laos, Vietnam, and southeastern China. The black head crest and white cheeks are telltale characteristics of the species.**

AGILE or DARK-HANDED GIBBON

(Hylobates agilis)

Gibbons are the smallest of the apes. Called lesser apes, their anatomy, social behavior, and teeth help differentiate them from the great apes—the gorilla, orangutan, and chimpanzee. There are several species of gibbons. *H. agilis* inhabits the rain forests of Sumatra, northern mainland Malaysia, southwestern Borneo, and peninsular Thailand. Adding to the difficulty of identification, their coloration varies geographically. Born to sing and swing, gibbons brachiate rapidly through the forest canopy using their elongated arms and hands to swing from branch to branch. The speed with which they can move through the trees is remarkable. These agile apes prefer a diet of sugar-rich fruits and figs, but will also eat young leaves, insects, and birds' eggs to get adequate protein.

◊ **The expressive face of an agile or dark-handed gibbon is outlined in white. These energetic lesser apes are native to the rain forests of Southeast Asia, where their echoing calls at dawn reverberate through the canopy.**

CRESTED, BLACK, WHITE-CHEEKED, or CONCOLOR GIBBON

(Hylobates concolor leucogenys)

Crested or concolor gibbons are native to Vietnam, Laos, eastern Cambodia, and southeastern China. Their coloration varies by sex and geography. The males are black, the females buff-colored. In China the males are all black, in Vietnam they are black with beige cheeks, and in Laos, black with white cheeks. Adults weigh about fifteen to eighteen pounds, and females are slightly heavier than males. The bonded adult pair produces a loud territorial duet. The ascending great call of the female is punctuated by the high-pitched barks and booms of the male. The features of such duets differ among species and subspecies.

◊ **A pair of monogamous concolor gibbons from Southeast Asia make momentary contact beneath the canopy. This species shows dichromatism—color differences between the sexes. Here the male is black and the female a reddish beige.**

◊ **A female concolor gibbon rests for a moment with her infant. The young primate takes the opportunity to explore its arboreal habitat.**

⬠ A female concolor gibbon grooms her mate. Less than 6 percent of all primate species are monogamous; gibbons are among this group.

△ Dangling from a tree branch, a male concolor gibbon native to Vietnam demonstrates the art of brachiation. Note the reversible grip used by each hand.

LAR or WHITE-HANDED GIBBON
(Hylobates lar)

White-handed gibbons are an endangered species native to the rain forests of Thailand, northern Sumatra, and peninsular Malaysia. They are named after their white hands and feet, which are offset against dense fur ranging in color from light beige to dark brown or black. A single infant is born after a seven-month gestation period. Weaning occurs at about two years of age, with the interbirth interval averaging two and a half years.

Gibbons are monogamous, meaning they pair-bond for life. To help maintain their reproductive bond and defend their territory, the male and female of most species sing together. Their early morning duets ring through the forest as one territorial pair calls after another. Hoot calls produced by the male accent the female's great long-calls, which build to a shrieking crescendo as she branch-shakes at the top of a tree.

⇧ **Gibbons are arboreal acrobats. They dangle from branches using elongated arms and hands as hooks to swing arm-over-arm through the rain forest canopy. Their long arms can also be extended to counterbalance bipedal steps taken over the tops of large branches and, more rarely, on the ground.**

▷ **A lar gibbon demonstrates its ability to walk bipedally over short distances on the ground. However, a gibbon's graceful, long-limbed body is designed primarily for high-speed brachiation through the tree tops.**

◊ Leaping and swinging from branch to branch, a gibbon can brachiate more rapidly through the canopy than a person can run on the ground. This ability enables gibbons to quickly access temporary food resources and better defend their territorial boundaries.

◊ A common lar gibbon shows why this species is also called a white-handed gibbon. Throughout their range, gibbon populations are decreasing rapidly in the wild due to habitat loss and illegal hunting. Although they are protected by laws in the countries of origin, enforcement continues to be difficult.

⬦ A white-handed gibbon cradles her single infant in a lap of folded ams and legs. Unlike the great apes, gibbons do not build nests. They usually sleep sitting upright on rump pads of tough, horny skin. Precocious at birth, a young gibbon is able to cling to its mother's hair unaided as she leaps and swings through the trees high above the ground.

▽ Flexible to the point of envy, a white-handed gibbon strikes an agile pose. One minute extended, the next minute contracted into a ball, gibbons are a sight to behold as they rocket through the canopy.

MOLOCH, JAVAN, OR SILVERY GIBBON

(Hylobates moloch)

The moloch gibbon inhabits the rain forests of western Java. Both sexes are the same color: silvery-gray topped with a dark gray cap. Group size averages around four—the adult pair and their immature young. From five to six offspring will be produced by the pair during their twenty-year reproductive period. Unlike other male gibbons, moloch males do not sing very often. This leaves the female to defend the pair's territory with her resonant great calls. Birds and squirrels compete for the gibbon's frugivorous food supplies—large raptors are their primary predators. Continued exploitation of Asia's rain forests and native wildlife has endangered the moloch gibbon.

◠ Showing off her lithe, agile body, a female pileated gibbon drapes herself over several tree branches. Note the shape and position of the unique gibbon thumb, which allows for a wide range of hand motion. So equipped, these fast-moving primates appear to defy gravity as they rapidly brachiate through the trees.

◊ Dense silver-gray fur surrounds the doleful face of a moloch gibbon. Infants are cream-colored at birth but quickly darken to the adult color. Their extremely long forearms enable gibbons to swing from branch to branch through the tree tops.

PILEATED or CAPPED GIBBON
(Hylobates pileatus)

Pileated gibbons are primarily native to southeastern Thailand and western Cambodia, where they live in monogamous family groups. Like most gibbons, they are active for eight to ten hours each day, from dawn to late afternoon. Feeding and calling behavior is most intense in the morning, but foraging activity continues throughout the day in the main canopy. Gibbons use the emergent trees that tower above the canopy to rest, call, and sleep. Throughout their range, pileated gibbons are endangered because of habitat loss. Agricultural encroachment, commercial logging, and hunting have taken their toll on this lesser ape, as did bombing and defoliation during the Vietnam War.

◁ A female pileated gibbon contours her body to the fork of a tree. These lesser apes are some of the most graceful and acrobatic of all primates.

MÜLLER'S or GRAY GIBBON
(Hylobates muelleri)

All gibbons are tail-less with dense fur surrounding bare, black faces. Müller's gibbons are native to Borneo, where they are fully protected. They are thought to be one of the last gibbon species to differentiate when gibbons began to spread throughout Southeast Asia a million years ago. They range in color from brown to mouse-gray. Family size includes the monogamous adult pair and up to four dependent offspring. During the adults' morning duets, the female takes the lead. Each sex produces an individual, sequential song that interfaces in perfect syncopation with the other. These signature calls not only identify their species, but the individual callers and the boundaries of their family territory.

⌂ A contemplative Müller's gibbon sits on a tree branch in Borneo. Just as with people, Müller's gibbons experience intergenerational conflict between monogamous adult pairs and their maturing subadult offspring. Same-sex tensions mount until the subadult is finally encouraged to leave the natal group.

◁ With arms outstretched, a female Müller's gibbon walks bipedally across a log in Borneo. The shape of a gibbon's elongated feet and hands is specially designed to grip branches. In fact, the Latin name *Hylobates* means "dweller in the trees."

◊ The elongated hand of a Bornean orangutan *(Pongo pygmaeus pygmaeus)* is adapted for grabbing tree trunks and branches in the tropical rain forests. Like humans, orangutans also have distinctive fingerprints.

⌂ This portrait of a Bornean orangutan clearly illustrates why these great apes have been called the "old men of the forest." Not only are orangutans smart, but they can be delightfully mischievous. Together with humans, these intelligent great apes are classified in the family Hominidae.

BORNEAN ORANGUTAN

(Pongo pygmaeus pygmaeus)

There are two subspecies of orangutans, one native to Sumatra, the other to Borneo. Both inhabit primary tropical rain forests where they prefer soft fruits such as figs, durian, and mangos. If these fruits are unavailable, they also eat leaves, insects, bark, squirrels, birds, and bird eggs. During the day these big red apes often descend to the ground. At night they sleep in leafy nests constructed high in the trees. Orangutans are relatively unsocial. Their primary social structure consists of solitary adult males, solitary subadults of both sexes, and adult females with one or two young. The males bellow and branch-shake to keep prospective rivals away. Their resonant calls carry for a half mile, amplified by their laryngeal air sacs.

◊ A female Bornean orangutan hangs from a tree with her juvenile offspring. Young orangutans are weaned when they are around three years of age but often remain with their mother for several more years.

⬆ A Bornean orangutan sucks his foot while using one of his long, powerful arms to hang onto a skinny tree trunk. Only when their vice-like grip is applied to your leg or arm can you fully appreciate their sheer muscular strength.

◊ The circle of pale skin around the eyes identifies this Bornean orangutan as a juvenile. Her long arms, short legs, and feet and hands specially designed for grabbing branches are clearly visible, even as she reclines in the dirt.

⬆ The longest-lasting bonds among orangutans are between the female and her young. Here, an infant hugs its mother.

◊ Young orangutans spend a considerable amount of time in play. So engaged, a little red imp hangs by its arms from a tree in Borneo.

SUMATRAN ORANGUTAN

(Pongo pygmaeus abelii)

Sexual dimorphism is quite obvious in orangutans, with males weighing from 170 to 220 pounds or more, and females half that. In Sumatra, orangutans inhabit a remnant area of rain forest in the mountainous north-west. Adult males of this subspecies sport mustaches and beards, and have prominent throat sacs which they use to roar and bellow. Orangutans move slowly through the trees using all four limbs to distribute their weight and enormous hands and feet to grab branches in a vice-like grip. Unlike the knuckle-walking chimps and gorillas, orangutans fist-walk over the ground. Like their locomotion, orangutan reproduction is very slow. Female orangutans can take up to ten years to mature, and then have the longest interbirth interval of any primate species, ranging from five to eight years. Because of this, their repro-ductive output is very limited during the course of their twenty-year period of fertility.

◊ An infant Sumatran orangutan obligingly sticks his face in the lens for a portrait. Baby orangutans have elevated the pursuit of inventive, exploratory play to a fine art.

⌂ A female orangutan displays the teeth that help her process a diet of soft fruit augmented with leaves, insects, and small vertebrates. Female orangutans are often killed in the wild so that their infants can be kid-napped for the pet trade. This practice, coupled with long interbirth intervals, has contributed to the orangutans' endangered status.

◊ The fatty cheek flaps, moustache, and beard of this handsome red ape belong to a male orangutan from Sumatra. Adult males are primarily solitary except during opportunities to mate with a receptive female. Subadult males will often force unwilling partners to copulate.

mexico, central

The

The countries with the largest remaining tracts of rain forest are home to the vast majority of primates. Not surprisingly, Brazil tops the list with sixteen genera and seventy-six species, of which 50 percent are endemic. This is quite remarkable, considering that the entire Neotropical region contains sixteen genera and ninety-eight species of primates. The countries of Peru with twelve genera and thirty-two species, and Colombia with twelve genera and thirty-one species, are also critical to Neotropical primate conservation.

While rain forest species are difficult to see in the wild, it is possible to hear the locomotive-like roar of a group of howler monkeys, the morning duets of monogamous titi monkeys, and the chirping, bird-like twitters of tamarins and marmosets as they forage through the canopy. From the tiny sap-eating pygmy marmoset that can fit in the palm of one's hand to the large, cream-colored muriqui, the Neotropics are a primate wonderland. And—nowhere else can one find monkeys with prehensile tails.

SILVERY MARMOSET

(Callithrix argentata)

COMMON MARMOSET

(Callithrix jacchus)

Silvery marmosets are unusual because of their coloration and bare, hairless ears. They occur in at least three color phases. One race is covered with dark fur, another is all white with a dark tail, and the third is white with a cream-colored tail. The hairless ears make it possible to identify the dark form from other marmoset species. These small diurnal primates are highly adapted for life in the trees. Even their high-pitched calls sound bird-like as they move through the canopy.

Common marmosets inhabit remnant patches of coastal forest along Brazil's heavily populated Atlantic coast. Here, they live in extended family groups that include an adult pair and their offspring. Typical of all marmosets, they have claws rather than nails on their fingers and toes, which enable them to climb up and down vertical trunks. An unusual feature of marmoset social organization is that the young are not only tolerated within their natal groups after reaching sexual maturity, but their maturation may be manipulated and delayed by the parents, forcing older siblings to help care for younger ones.

⇧ The marbled tail and white ear tufts identify this primate as a common marmoset. These small South American monkeys locomote through the trees with jerky, squirrel-like motion.

⇧ The white hair, pink face, and elfin ears on this little primate identify it as a silvery marmoset native to the rain forests of South America.

◇ **Black ear-tufted marmosets are a subspecies of the common marmoset. Their white face and black-and-gray-marbled tail and body fur show the relationship.**

PYGMY MARMOSET
(Cebuella pygmaea)

BLACK EAR-TUFTED MARMOSET
(Callithrix penicillata)

Pygmy marmosets are the quietest of New World monkeys—and the smallest. Adults weigh a little more than two to three ounces, and measure five inches long with an eight-inch tail. These tiny primates live in the rain forests and seasonally flooded forests of the upper Amazon Basin in Brazil, Colombia, Ecuador, Peru, and northern Bolivia. In addition to high-pitched whistles and twitters, pygmy marmosets also produce an ultrasonic cry expressing hostility that is inaudible to the human ear.

For all intents and purposes, marmosets and tamarins look alike. They are both small, diurnal New World monkeys. However, the anatomy of their lower jaws helps to tell them apart: Tamarins have more rounded lower jaws, while marmosets have more pointed, V-shaped jaws to accommodate their chisel-shaped lower incisors. This difference enables marmosets, like the black ear-tufted subspecies, to gouge holes in the bark of trees to extract resins, gums, and sap. Marmosets produce a variety of high-pitched vocalizations, some inaudible to the human ear. They also perform elaborate visual displays, raising and lowering the hair on their tail, face, and tufted ears.

◇ **Cupped in the palm of a human hand, a pygmy marmoset from South America seems even further dwarfed in size. It is one of the world's smallest species of primates.**

◊ **Pygmy marmosets make every effort to stay out of sight. Their cryptic coloration and small size make this possible, along with movement that includes squirrel-like dashes, sloth-like oozing over tree trunks, and abrupt frozen immobility.**

EMPEROR TAMARIN

(Saguinus imperator subgriscescens)

The emperor tamarin's bold, drooping white mustache is typical of the decorative pattern of facial hair common to tamarin species. Such eye-catching patterns are thought to emphasize social displays. The disruptive coloration may also help to camouflage these primates in their rain forest habitats. Tamarins exploit all levels of the forest in search of fruit and insects. While foraging, they run along large branches and make short horizontal jumps between tree trunks and low shrubs. Groups ranging in size from two to forty have been observed.

⌂ A male emperor tamarin carries his twin infants on his back. Marmosets and tamarins usually give birth to twins.

GOLDEN-HANDED TAMARIN

(Saguinus midas midas)

Golden-handed tamarins are classified as one of the "hairy-faced" tamarins. They inhabit tropical rain forests north of the Rio Amazonas in South America. Like all tamarins, this species makes a variety of high-pitched shrieks, squeals, trills, and twitters, many of which the human ear can't hear. Infants make sounds to request food. Golden-handed tamarins occur in groups of ten or less. If more than one adult female is present, only the most dominant breeds. These small-bodied primates feed on fruits, small invertebrates, and insects.

⌂ **The brightly colored hands and feet on this tamarin distinguish it as a golden-handed tamarin. Subspecies distinctions are based on the color of the hands and feet, which can range from golden-orange to black.**

SPIX'S MOUSTACHED TAMARIN

(Saguinus mystax mystax)

⌂ **An inquisitive moustached tamarin shows off its namesake white facial hair. Such dramatic markings serve as both visual signals and species I.D. tags as these high-energy little primates move through the canopy.**

Moustached tamarins use their clawed digits for quadrupedal running along branches, horizontal jumps between tree trunks, and for prolonged bouts of social grooming. Running their claws through each other's fur, they comb out unwanted particles and remove them with lips, teeth, and tongue. There is no sexual dimorphism among adult tamarins; both have muzzles of bright white facial hair. If anything, the females can be slightly larger than the males.

▽ The white crown, reddish rump, and black-tipped tail make cotton-top tamarins one of the most striking species of New World primates. They are named for the crest of long white hair that flows from their head down over their shoulders. The crest is raised and lowered to accentuate their facial expressions and twittering vocalizations.

COTTON-TOP TAMARIN

(Saguinus oedipus)

Cotton-top tamarins are an endangered species found only in Colombia. They make twittering bird-like calls to each other as they move through their preferred habitat, the tangled forest understory of low-growing trees and vines. Their vocalizations also include louder trills and shrieks produced over territorial disputes and when predators are near. Twins are born after a gestation period of four to five months. The male is the primary caregiver. He carries the infants on his back, returning them to the female when they need to nurse. Group size ranges from three to thirteen individuals.

GOLDEN LION TAMARIN

(Leontopithecus rosalia)

GEOFFROY'S TAMARIN

(Saguinus geoffroyi)

This small Neotropical primate is the most northern-ranging of the tamarin species. Once found throughout most of Panama into northwest Colombia, Geoffroy's tamarins have since been eliminated over much of their former range. Field studies show that this diurnal primate prefers to forage for fruit, insects, and various plant material in second-growth habitats during midmorning and late afternoon. At night, family groups consisting of a monogamous adult pair and their off-spring sleep hidden in vine tangles.

The golden lion tamarin is native to the coastal rain forests of eastern Brazil. Weighing about three-quarters to one and a half pounds, it is the largest of the callitrichid primates (marmosets and tamarins). Their common name is derived from the gold, lion-like mane that covers their outer ears and extends like a cape over their shoulders. Males have well-developed laryngeal air sacs. When angry, lion tamarins expose their canines while producing shrill whistles and shrieks. Under calmer circumstances, adults use other calls to invite their young to eat, even offering them food.

◁ **A Geoffroy's tamarin shows off its distinctive color pattern—a salt-and-pepper back, reddish nape, white forearms and underparts, and black face with short white hairs on top of its head.**

▷ **Golden lion tamarins are native to the Atlantic coastal forests of eastern Brazil, where the climate alternates between wet and dry seasons. By day, these endangered primates actively search vines and lianas for their diet of insects, spiders, and fruit.**

GOLDEN-HEADED LION TAMARIN

(Leontopithecus chrysomelas)

The golden-headed lion tamarin differs from the other species of lion tamarins by its golden-red face, forelimbs, and upper tail. These little primates are as beautiful as they are rare. Remnant populations survive in just a few isolated pockets of rain forest left along Brazil's eastern coast. Lion tamarins communicate with each other through a rich repertoire of vocalizations. They also use several scent-marking glands to produce chemical signals. Lion tamarins, like other tamarin species, use their long, thin tails to help them balance as they move through the trees.

◁ **The facial hair of this golden-headed lion tamarin from Brazil looks as if it has been painted. In addition to their namesake manes, all lion tamarins have noticably elongated digits, with the middle digit twice as long as the width of the palm.**

GOELDI'S MONKEY

(Callimico goeldii)

Native to the tropical forests from Colombia to Bolivia, Goeldi's monkeys move rapidly through the lower canopy by vertically clinging and leaping. These beautiful little primates are covered with long, silky black hair. In size and shape, Goeldi's resembles other marmosets, but their teeth are more tamarin-like than marmoset. In fact, this species was given its own genus because it combines marmoset features with those of tamarins and other New World monkeys. Their reproductive pattern also strays from that of marmosets. Following a gestation period of five to five and a half months, the female gives birth to a single infant, not twins. The mother carries the infant for the first two weeks of life, then transfers that responsibility to the father.

⬦ A Goeldi's monkey from South America grimaces at the photographer's intrusion. This snub-nosed little primate has become a rare species due to habitat loss and capture for the pet trade.

◊ Twinning is rare among the arboreal capuchin monkeys of Central and South America. Here, a brown pale-fronted capuchin infant clings tightly to its mother.

WHITE-FRONTED or
BROWN PALE-FRONTED CAPUCHIN

(Cebus albifrons)

Capuchin monkeys are one of the most wide-ranging of New World primates. They are also extremely intelligent, with noticeably large, convoluted brains relative to body weight. At home in a variety of forest types, the fruit-eating capuchin monkeys often rest with their legs and arms dangling from a branch, their prehensile tail tips securely anchored. Averaging six pounds, these quadrupedal springers are adept at using their hands to forage for food. Opposable thumbs and keen eye-to-hand coordination enable capuchins to pick up the tiniest objects with great precision. This trait, among others, made capuchins appealing as organ-grinder monkeys in the streets of Boston and New York early this century. Along with grabbing fruit, they also learned how to grab coins.

TUFTED or BLACK-CAPPED CAPUCHIN

(Cebus apella)

With black hands and feet, head tufts that form a triangle over their foreheads, and distinctive black sideburns extending to the chin, the tufted capuchin is an engaging monkey. Living in groups of five to twenty individuals, these New World monkeys communicate with grins, lowered eyebrows, head-shaking, and a variety of calls. Native to the rain forests of South America, the omnivorous capuchins use their semi-prehensile tails to balance as they locomote through the trees. Males are larger than females, yet it is the female who decides when to mate—and with whom. At the peak of receptivity, she follows the dominant male. As receptivity wanes, she pursues the subordinate males, copulating with as many as six in a day.

⌂ The tufted or black-capped capuchin is a medium-sized monkey native to South America. Although primarily tree-dwelling, they frequently descend to the ground to raid crops and orchards. Fond of palmnuts, tufted capuchins use special nutcracking techniques, such as banging them against branches to remove the nutmeat. They are also adept at catching and eating tree frogs.

◊ Capuchin monkeys have been called the hustlers of the American primate world. When a group forages for food, they spread out throughout the canopy to systematically search for everything edible. Here a white-faced capuchin monkey intently manipulates a flower blossom in search of insects.

WHITE-FACED or WHITE-THROATED CAPUCHIN

(Cebus capucinus)

Both in the wild and captivity, capuchin monkeys are entertaining to watch. They energetically explore their environment using their semi-prehensile tails as anchors when they feed and rest. In captivity, white-faced capuchins explore everything they can reach, often taking things apart in the process. Easily bored in captivity, their short attention spans reflect both their intelligence and their rapid search-and-explore foraging techniques, ideal for the stimulus-rich rain forests of South and Central America.

⇧ **The agile, intelligent capuchin monkeys roam over fairly large rain forest territories, through which they move rapidly in search of food. They play an important role in the forest ecology by pollinating flowers and dispersing seeds as they go.**

NIGHT MONKEY or DOUROCOULI
(Aotus sp.)

/ The Latin name *Aotus* is used as often as dourocouli or night monkey to describe this New World primate. These arboreal, two-pound monkeys inhabit a variety of forest types from Panama to Paraguay and Argentina. Their diet consists mostly of fruit. Like their diurnal counterparts, the titi monkeys, dourocouli live in monogamous family groups of a mated pair and their one to three young. Asleep by day and active after dusk, night monkeys use elaborate visual, vocal, and olfactory signals to communicate with each other, including a series of resonating grunts produced in their laryngeal sacs.

▽ The dourocouli, native to South America, is also called the owl or night monkey. Its enormous eyes are an adaptation for seeing well in the dark. This species has the distinction of being the only Neotropical primate that is completely nocturnal.

◊ Male dourocouli, or night monkeys, actively participate in raising their young. Here an infant rides on the back of its devoted father. Only when it gets hungry will it be returned to the female to nurse.

DUSKY TITI MONKEY

(Callicebus donacophilus)

Dusky titi monkeys are one of three species of titi monkeys native to the tropical rain forests of South America. This particular species prefers dense swamp forests. These small, day-active monkeys supplement their mostly fruit diet with leaves and insects. Titi monkeys are one of the few species of primates that live in monogamous family groups, each with a mated adult pair and their young. Like gibbons, the male and female produce territorial duets or dawn calls. When resting or sleeping, they tail-twine. Male titi monkeys are devoted fathers. They carry, groom, guard, share food with, and play with their infant, even sheltering it from wind and rain.

⌂ Balancing on a palm frond, a squirrel monkey demonstrates its quadrupedal movement through the trees. This agile species is adept at collecting berry-like fruit from the ends of branches.

⌂ Dusky titi monkeys from South America range in color from reddish-brown to gray. As is true for most monogamous primates, sexual dimorphism is minimal.

SQUIRREL MONKEY

(Saimiri sp.)

Squirrel monkeys live throughout most of the tropical rain forests of the northern Amazon Basin. Here, they prefer the middle canopy to forage for fruit and insects. They also eat snails, arthropods, and small vertebrates such as tree frogs. Owners of fruit orchards in the Amazon region consider this species a pest. Male squirrel monkeys are unusual among primates for becoming "fatted"—putting on weight in the upper torso—during the breeding season. Males also use penile displays during this time to help maintain dominance hierarchies. Group size can vary from ten to more than two hundred individuals in undisturbed Amazon rain forests.

▽ **Unlike many species of Neotropical monkeys, the tails of squirrel monkeys are not prehensile, even though at times they may appear so.**

◁ **A squirrel monkey takes a siesta on a branch in a South American rain forest. Squirrel monkeys show little sexual dimorphism in size or color.**

WHITE-FACED SAKI

(Pithecia pithecia pithecia)

Saki monkeys are medium-sized South American primates that inhabit the rain forests of the Amazon Basin. Striking sexual dimorphism occurs in the white-faced saki. The male is completely black except for a dramatic white mask of short dense hair surrounding his black muzzle. In contrast, the female is much lighter with brown to brownish-gray fur and a gold chest and underbelly. In both sexes, the head hair grows forward from the nape of the neck to form a hood. Saki monkeys live in monogamous family groups. The adult pair maintains their bond through grooming and coordinated vocal duets.

◊ **A male white-faced saki monkey shows the striking sexual dimorphism characteristic of this species. Only the male has the white mask.**

△ **Female white-faced saki monkeys can easily be mistaken for the Monk saki. Both species inhabit the rain forests of the Amazon Basin, where their springing, leaping locomotion through the trees has given them the nickname "flying monkeys."**

RED UAKARI
(Cacajao rubicundus)

MANTLED HOWLER MONKEY
(Alouatta palliata)

Uakaris are medium-sized monkeys native to the tropical rain forests of the upper Amazon Basin. Their range extends from southern Venezuela to eastern Peru. These strange-looking monkeys have several features unique among New World monkeys. Most obvious are their bald heads with bare crimson faces. Their long shaggy fur, either all white or reddish-brown, exaggerates the dramatic visual effect created by their hairless red heads. To further enhance their appeal to females, male uakaris urine-wash. This gives each one a distinctive, signature odor.

◁ **Even a makeup artist would be hard-pressed to match the visual effect created naturally by a red uakari from South America. Loss of habitat has made this showstopper primate vulnerable. They are also hunted for their meat and are even used as fishing bait.**

Howler monkeys are the most widespread of all New World primates. Various species occur from southern Mexico to Brazil and Argentina. Like all howlers, the mantled howler of Central and South America is completely arboreal. They move quadrupedally through the middle and upper stories of the forest canopy aided by their prehensile tails. Both sexes possess an enlarged, egg-shaped hyoid bone just beneath the chin, which is used to produce their deep roaring vocalizations. Howlers call at dawn, during territorial disputes, and in response to loud noise, such as heavy rainfall.

▷ **Mantled howler monkeys are arboreal New World primates native to Central and South America. This species is seriously threatened throughout its range because of hunting, habitat loss, and pesticide use.**

RED HOWLER MONKEY

(Alouatta seniculus)

It's obvious why these New World monkeys are called red howlers. Their beautiful coats range from red to brownish-orange, and their roaring group calls can make the air vibrate. Red howlers call in unison throughout the day and night. Territorial encounters with other groups usually set off a chorus, but so will just about any other loud sound, including that of a motorcycle. Group size ranges from three to thirteen or more. Competition for the few breeding positions within a group is intense, both among females and among males. Able to survive in a variety of forest types, including secondary growth, howlers are completely arboreal. However, if given a choice, they prefer to feed and rest in the middle and upper canopies of primary forests.

◊ **A red howler monkey peers from the canopy in a Venezuelan forest. Field scientists learn quickly not to walk directly beneath a howler monkey, since these calculating monkeys know how to use their body fluids to discourage approach.**

▽ **The large swelling beneath the chin, needed to accommodate an enlarged hyoid bone, is concealed by the thick beard on this Mexican black or Guatemalan howler monkey. The hyoid bone makes it possible for howler monkeys to produce a loud, deep call, which they often do in unison, resembling the roar of a passing locomotive.**

MEXICAN BLACK or GUATEMALAN HOWLER MONKEY

(Alouatta pigra)

All howler monkeys are hind-gut fermenters. They rely on stomach bacteria to break down the plant cellulose consumed in their diet of low-nutrient, low-sugar leaves and unripe fruit. The poor nutritional content of their food means that they must consume huge quantities to get adequate nutrition. Their lethargic behavior when not feeding is a behavioral byproduct of their long, slow digestive process. Guatemalan howlers inhabit the undisturbed tropical and semideciduous forests of Central America. However, such forests are now largely gone, and along with them the black howling monkeys with their prehensile tails.

LONG-HAIRED SPIDER MONKEY

(Ateles belzebuth)

Long-haired spider monkeys are native to the tropical evergreen forests from northern Colombia and Venezuela to northern Peru. They use their prehensile tails like a fifth limb to dangle upside-down from branches while feeding, and to move in every position possible through the canopy. Holding their tails aloft, they occasionally walk bipedally across large branches. Nearly 80 percent of a spider monkey's diet is fruit; the rest is leaves. These animated monkeys bark, scream, grunt, squeak, hoot, wail, and moan. Urine and glandular secretions help them communicate through olfactory signals.

◊ **A young long-haired spider monkey from South America has the best hammock of all—its mother. Her prehensile tail makes it possible for her to nonchalantly dangle, leaving one long, spidery arm free. Also visible is her long, pendulous clitoris which resembles a male penis. This trait, shared with female howler and woolly spider monkeys, often makes it difficult to differentiate the sexes in the wild.**

⌂ A black-handed spider monkey stands bipedally on a tree branch to get a better look at the view. The pink patches of skin encircling the eyes give it a spectacled appearance.

◊ A black-handed spider monkey demonstrates "feeding by tail." Naked skin on the lower third of the prehensile tail enables this fifth appendage to tightly grip branches. Just like a hand, the tail has sweat glands, sensory nerve endings, and "fingerprints."

⌂ A female black-handed spider monkey opens her mouth to make a threatening vocalization. This species has been introduced to Panama's Barro Colorado Island.

◇ **Black-handed spider monkeys come in a variety of colors. Here a female shows off her reddish, pot-bellied undersides, while her pink-faced infant watches. Notice that a spider monkey's hands are thumbless. A tubercle takes the place of the missing digit.**

BLACK-HANDED
SPIDER MONKEY

(Ateles geoffroyi vellerosus)

Black-handed spider monkeys can be red, buff, golden, or dark brown with black patches on their head, hands, and feet. Nine to fifteen subspecies have been identified. The most permanent social bonds are between females and their dependent young. Although there is no marked sexual dimorphism among spider monkeys, female skulls tend to be slightly larger than male skulls, with the inverse true for their canines. Spider monkeys exhibit a fission-fusion pattern of social organization. Larger groups break down into smaller foraging units by day, during which members are exchanged throughout the day.

▽ Surrounded by a sea of black fur, an infant black spider monkey peeks at the world from the security of his mother. This Neotropical species prefers the canopy of moist evergreen forests, where it eats mostly fruit.

BLACK SPIDER MONKEY

(Ateles fusciceps robustus)

The black spider monkeys of Central and South America move through the canopy with speed and agility, brachiating and running over the branches in search of ripe fruit. These large, lanky, and noticeably pot-bellied primates live in groups averaging eighteen individuals. The groups are centered on the females and their young. Female spider monkeys actively choose their mates. While some females may choose to mate with several different males in a single day, other female-directed pairings can last up to three days. Black spider monkeys copulate face-to-face, as do gibbons, bonobos, orangutans, capuchins, and a few other primate species.

◁ A black spider monkey infant uses his hands, feet, and prehensile tail to hold onto its mother. Considered good to eat, these monkeys have been severely hunted throughout their range.

MURIQUI or WOOLLY SPIDER MONKEY

(Brachyteles arachnoides)

The muriqui, also called a woolly spider monkey, is a large South American primate that looks part spider monkey, part woolly monkey. Like the spider monkeys, it has long, spider-like limbs and vestigial thumbs. Like a woolly monkey, it has short dense fur and a more rounded head. Muriqui have a rich repertoire of vocalizations, including clucks, neighs, warbles, chuckles, and loud barks. Touching, especially embraces between group members, also plays an important part in their social behavior. This slow-breeding, highly endangered species lives in the tropical rain forests along the southeastern coast of Brazil. Habitat destruction reduced their numbers to less than 1,000 in the 1970s.

⬢ **The brownish-yellow fur and intelligent face of a muriqui clearly shows in this portrait. Found only in Brazil, these twenty-four- to thirty-pound monkeys are the largest species of Neotropical primates.**

The bare undersurface of the woolly monkey's prehensile tail is covered with dermatoglyphics or fingerprints, which function like tread on a rubber tire. The primates use their super-grip tails to swing, dangle, and grab branches as they feed, rest, and move through the trees.

WOOLLY MONKEY

(Lagothrix lagotricha)

The common woolly monkey inhabits the middle and upper Amazon Basin. They forage through all levels of the canopy in tropical and montane forests, where they feed on ripe fruits and leaves. Woolly monkeys can be brown, gray, or black in color. Field identification of the sexes is difficult because the female clitoris is conspicuous and often longer than the male penis. Woolly monkeys live in groups averaging ten to twelve members, with larger groups forming in nonhunted areas. In addition to suffering habitat loss, woolly monkeys are captured for the pet trade and relished as a food item—their fat is used in cooking and medicine.

◊ **A woolly monkey poses for the camera, showing off the wonderful lines and contours of its human-like face. Their dense short hair, snub noses, and long prehensile tails are characteristic of the species. These large New World monkeys eat mostly fruit.**

1. Burton, Frances, and Matthew Eaton. 1995. **THE MULTIMEDIA GUIDE TO THE NON-HUMAN PRIMATES.** New York: Prentice Hall.

2. Burton, John, and Bruce Pearson. 1987. **THE COLLINS GUIDE TO THE RARE MAMMALS OF THE WORLD.** London: William Collins Sons, Ltd.

3. Cheney, Dorothy, and Robert Seyfarth. 1990. **HOW MONKEYS SEE THE WORLD: INSIDE THE MIND OF ANOTHER SPECIES.** Chicago: University of Chicago Press.

4. Dorst, Jean, and Tierre Dandelot. 1972. **A FIELD GUIDE TO THE LARGER MAMMALS OF AFRICA.** London: William Collins Sons, Ltd.

5. Eisenberg, John. 1989. **MAMMALS OF THE NEOTROPICS: THE NORTHERN NEOTROPICS, VOL. 1.** Chicago: University of Chicago Press.

6. Emmons, Louise. 1990. **NEOTROPICAL RAINFOREST MAMMALS: A FIELD GUIDE.** Chicago: University of Chicago Press.

7. Fossey, Dian. 1983. **GORILLAS IN THE MIST.** Boston: Houghton Mifflin.

8. Glaw, Frank, and Miguel Vences. 1994. **A FIELD GUIDE TO THE AMPHIBIANS AND REPTILES OF MADAGASCAR INCLUDING MAMMALS AND FRESH-WATER FISH.** Cologne, Germany: Moosdruck, Leverkusen and Farbo.

9. Goodall, Jane. 1986. **THE CHIMPANZEES OF GOMBE: PATTERNS OF BEHAVIOR.** Cambridge: Belknap Press of Harvard.

10. Haltenorth, Theodor. 1984. **A FIELD GUIDE TO THE MAMMALS OF AFRICA INCLUDING MADAGASCAR.** London: William Collins Sons, Ltd.

11. Kavanagh, Michael. 1984. **A COMPLETE GUIDE TO MONKEYS, APES, AND OTHER PRIMATES.** New York: Viking Press.

12. Mittermeier, Russell A., Ian Tattersall, William Konstant, David Meyers, and Roderic Mast. 1994. **LEMURS OF MADAGASCAR.** Washington, D.C.: Conservation International.

13. Moynihan, Martin. 1976. **THE NEW WORLD PRIMATES.** Princeton: Princeton University Press.

14. Napier, J. R. and P. H. 1994. **THE NATU-RAL HISTORY OF PRIMATES.** Cambridge: MIT Press.

15. Nowak, Ronald M., and John L. Paradiso. 1991. **WALKER'S MAMMALS OF THE WORLD.** Baltimore: Johns Hopkins University Press.

16. Preston-Mafham, Rod and Ken. 1992. **PRIMATES OF THE WORLD.** New York: Facts on File.

17. Roonwal, M.L., and S. M. Mohnot. 1977. **PRIMATES OF SOUTH ASIA: ECOLOGY, SOCIOBIOLOGY, AND BEHAVIOR.** Cambridge: Harvard University Press.

18. Smuts, B., D. Cheeney, R. Seyfarth, R. Wrangham, and T. Struhsaker (eds.). 1987. **PRIMATE SOCIETIES.** Chicago: University of Chicago Press.

19. Wolfheim, Jaclyn. 1983. **PRIMATES OF THE WORLD: DISTRIBUTION, ABUN-DANCE, AND CONSERVATION.** Seattle: University of Washington Press.

BARBARA SLEEPER

I wish to thank the following people:

Dr. Joan Lockard for serving as both advisor and mentor during my studies of human and nonhuman primatology at the University of Washington; Dr. Pelham Aldrich-Blake for providing the opportunity to study sympatric primate species in the tropical rain forests of central Malaysia; Dr. Warren G. Kinzey for organizing the numerous expeditions to Peru to study yellow-handed titi monkeys, and the rare opportunity to search for the masked titi monkey and muriqui in Brazil; and Regina Frey and Monica Borner for the insights gained while living with orangutans at the Bohorek rehabilitation station in Sumatra.

For review of the primate facts presented in this book, Russell A. Mittermeier, Chairman of the IUCN/SSC Primate Specialist Group and President of Conservation International; Gary M. Stolz, Chief Naturalist with the U.S. Fish and Wildlife Service; and Dr. Shirley McGreal of the International Primate Protection League. The author also acknowledges the many field scientists who have painstakingly gleaned the available primate natural history data from months and years of patient observation in the field.

Thanks go to Art Wolfe for capturing the wondrous world of primates in his series of beautiful photographs, and to his staff, Christine Eckhoff, Deirdre Skillman, Mel Calvan, Ray Pfortner, Gavriel Jecan, and Craig Scheak for their assistance during this project.

Special acknowledgment goes to my daughter, Kelly Citron, who provided invaluable help as a research assistant during preparation of the text, and to my sons, Josh and David Citron, for providing amusing distractions. Thanks also go to Bob Citron for his technical wizardry with online computer systems, and his critical help with child care needed to complete the text.

Special thanks go to friends Jan Wagner, Tom Boyden, Helen Rodway, Alta Baller, Steve Muth, and Mandy Will for their perpetual encouragement; and to fellow primate-lovers Carol Rivero, Carol Neimeyer, Carol Fahrenbruch, Lynn Hynes, Barbara Kirkevold, and Sorella Siboni who have been there since the beginning.

Finally, I give thanks to my parents, Norma and Bill Sleeper, for encouragement to follow the road less traveled, and to my brother, Bill Sleeper, and wife, Lynne Evans-Sleeper, for being role models of accomplishment—with humor and humility.

Art and I would both like to thank Christina Wilson and Martine Trélaün, designer, both at Chronicle Books.

ART WOLFE ◊

Among those who shared my travels and assisted me along the way, I want to thank Gavriel Jecan, James and Teri Martin, Donna Naruo, Ian MacKenzie, and Roxanne Kremer.

For their permission and assistance with research and arrangements to photograph, my sincere and deep appreciation to Mike Lockyer and Ernie Thesford, Howletts and Port Lympne—The John Aspinall Zoo Parks and Gardens, England; Bernard Harrison, Singapore Zoological Gardens, Singapore; Khun Sopoj Methaphivat, Chiang Mai Zoo, Thailand; Khun Sophon Dumnui, Khao Kheow Open Zoo, Thailand; Smithsonian Research Center Facility, Barro Colorado Island, Panama; Boston Zoo, Massachusetts; St. Louis Zoo, Missouri; Linda Corcoran, Bronx Zoo, New York; Cincinnati Zoo, Ohio; San Francisco Zoo, The Zoological Society of San Diego, and Deborah Levy, Los Angeles Zoo, California; Phoenix Zoo, Arizona; Harmony Frazier, Janice Joslin, Linda Shipe, and Paula Brady, Woodland Park Zoo, Washington; Kenneth Glander and David Haring, Duke University Primate Center, North Carolina; George Small, Smithsonian Research Facility—Mpala Ranch, Kenya; Cathy Delaney, University of Washington Primate Research Center, Washington; Gary Stolz, U.S. Fish and Wildlife Service, United States Department of Interior, Washington, D.C; and Dr. Russell Mittermeier, Conservation International, Washington, D.C.

Of all the many people connected to this book, the ones who stand out are those who made it possible from the beginning to the end. I'd like to thank the staff of Art Wolfe, Inc.— Deirdre Skillman, Craig Scheak, Ray Pfortner, Gavriel Jecan, Christine Eckhoff, and Mel Calvan.